WHERE DARKNESS LIVES &

OTHER MONSTROUS TALES:
An Anthology of Fantasy, Horror
and Speculative Flash Fiction

WHERE DARKNESS LIVES &

OTHER MONSTROUS TALES:
An Anthology of Fantasy, Horror and Speculative Flash Fiction

MINUTE FICTION
VOLUME #2

Minute Fiction

ISBN-13: 978-1-7323323-3-1
ISBN: 1-7323323-3-1

Cover art: Raun Edano
Illustrations: Robin Edano and Raun Edano
Special thanks to Annette Corkey

Printed in the United States of America
First Edition

TABLE OF CONTENTS

INTRODUCTION

The gods made man, and man made monsters.

I've always been fascinated by monsters. Bizarre creatures in shape and manner with few limits on either, they feel like concentrations of magic so wondrous that your imagination has no choice but to grow if it wants to wrap around them. In the same moment, they can be the stuff of nightmares, silhouetted against your window after you were foolish enough to turn off the light. Monsters are entertainment, explanations and warnings—don't venture too far off the path, or something will gobble you up.

Happily, I'm in good company: I was lucky enough to see Guillermo del Toro's "At Home with Monsters" exhibit when it came to California in 2016, and have often found myself parked outside my home after work, finishing an episode of Aaron Mahnke's *Lore* podcast. Both portray monsters in ways that are unmistakably their own: Del Toro's creatures burst with color and tower in the imagination, while Mahnke's dissections of werewolf and wendigo myths fill you with creeping dread.

But perhaps more fascinating than their methods is the way they treat their subjects: with kindness. Del Toro is just as likely to write about benign ghosts or a lovesick fishman as he is the eyeball-handed Pale Man. Mahnke's retellings of monster myths are sympathetic to the creatures at their core, often highlighting how human failings led to their creation.

We lay the blame for a thousand horrors on the shoulders of monsters, from shipwrecks to illness to children gone missing in the woods. It seems harmless until the monster is made real: villagers in Salem who suffered from food poisoning accused vulnerable women of "bewitching" them, and in Europe, developmentally disabled children were once dubbed "changelings" and left in forests to die. And, often enough, we explain away the unthinkable cruelty of humans by attributing it to a monster—the first, bloodthirsty werewolf was nothing more than a man in wolf's clothing, after all.

So what is a monster? A horrific, murderous demon, or a misunderstood beast?

I would say it can be both.

Humans created monsters as vessels for our own cruelties and failings. However, you can't escape yourself so easily, and our creations have taken on more than just the worst of us. They are our reflections in a different shape, with virtues as clear as their imperfections. A monster's story can just as easily be a horror, a cautionary tale, a comedy, or a romance, because they're made in our image.

I'm not asking you to find the *real* monsters hidden in this book, because the difference between a human and a monster can be as slight as a few misplaced scales. Instead, I hope you step wholeheartedly into these monster tales and truly meet the creatures within, from a thoughtful spider to a naive harpy to a world-swallowing behemoth. I hope that, when you do, you find creatures as varied and complex as we are.

The Del Toro exhibit opens with a quote that encompasses his philosophy: "I love monsters, I identify with monsters." We could all stand to open our hearts so readily to the unfamiliar, the mute, and the misunderstood—perhaps we'd find it all less frightening.

Ashley Reed
August 2019

THE SERPENT'S TALE

Today was the day he'd kill the beast.

Ean crouched in the rushes at the spring's edge, the trickle of water piercing the windless quiet. The old willow draped over the spring like a creature bending to drink. Huddled in the green shade beneath its canopy, he waited, knives warming between his fingers.

Everyone knew the beast that lurked in the willow spring could drain the blood of a full-grown warrior. Every night, stories of its slitted eyes, the hunters it felled, and the treasure it guarded danced through the campfire sparks. The matriarchs each insisted it protected something different: silt-bound metals, healing waters, succulent fish that gave everlasting life. *Something precious.*

He would be the one to claim it.

The grass near the willow's roots shivered. A water bird, perhaps, or a frog, as it had been the last dozen times. But something greater rose from the shallows: a hulking shadow, obsidian scales gleaming under streaming rivulets. It stretched until its head met the bowing branches, twice as tall and twice as thick as the village's largest man.

Ean's mouth dropped open. The knife slipped from his hand and split the quiet with a splash.

Two yellow eyes fixed on him in an instant; a dozen more opened like bubbles bursting in a swamp. From deep in its throat came a rumbling growl.

Ean stumbled back, boots sinking into the mud. With a howl, he flung the other three knives—his aim was true, the tips piercing the snake's flesh.

But it didn't flinch. Its growl caught and puffed out in bursts. It was—*laughing*.

"Ah, what great warrior comes to fell me today?" the serpent chuckled, voice pounding like a drum. Its great muscles roiled and the knives tumbled away like harmless burrs. "Have you just grown out of your swaddling clothes?"

Ean's face flashed hot. "I'm ten turns!" he yelled indignantly.

"It's not worth the effort to eat you. All bones for no meat," the beast said, shaking its massive head as it slithered out of the water. "Run along, little kit. I won't be so kind next time."

It vanished into the trees as if it never was, leaving Ean gaping.

Today was the day he'd kill the beast.

He perched in a tree at the spring's edge. The willow had grown in the last decade and nearly shaded the entire spring. All but two of the elders had passed, yet they still chortled through tales of young Ean's inglorious retreat from this place to any children who would listen. This time would be different.

"Hmm," came that familiar, thrumming voice, but not from the water. Ean pivoted, gripping his spear tightly. The beast blinked at him as it slid out of the forest. "You look bigger than the last time we met, kit."

"You look smaller," Ean snapped. The willow beast was colossal, but no longer towered over him and did not look so daunting as it once had.

"As is the way of things. I warned you what would happen if you returned." Its mouth drifted open, rows of jagged teeth stretching into its throat.

Before Ean could spit back something clever, the beast lunged. He danced away from its jaw, but the beast was too fast, spinning and slamming its skull into his chest. He crashed to the ground, its teeth closing on his shoulder like a bear trap.

Ean roared, blood pouring down his arm, and plunged the spear into its eye. Hissing in agony, the beast flailed and flung him into the muddy shallows.

When he sat up, gasping for breath, it was to uproarious laughter. "You've grown stronger," the beast said as Ean wrapped shaking fingers around his shoulder. "But one man cannot kill me. Fight me day and night—no weapon will be my end."

The beast slithered into the spring and out of sight, leaving Ean to bleed in silence.

Today was the day he'd kill the beast.

He strode into the clearing, listening for any hint of movement. The matriarchs had passed and taken their stories with them; his shoulders had grown wide and his beard thick. But this place hadn't changed: the pool was clear as the day he first set eyes upon it.

He knew what else hadn't changed. "Beast!" he bellowed, birds screeching as they darted from the reeds. He drew his spear from the clasps on his back—he couldn't stomach the firearms the young men hunted with these days, reeking of smoke and gunpowder. "You may have bested a child, but what will you make of a man?"

Only trickling water answered. Or, no—his ears pricked as he heard that blood-boiling chuckle. But it was slight, a flutter on the breeze.

"Well met, kit."

Ean whirled, finding nothing but foliage until he looked to the willow's branches. A thin tuft of blackness hung there like moss; only after he stepped close did he see a dozen yellow eyes looking back at him.

He stilled, his mind gone quiet. The beast seemed to understand his thoughts before he did.

"Ah, I'll have none of your pity," the willow beast said. It was barely the size of a water snake, deep black skin now a wrinkled gray.

"What . . .?" Ean breathed.

It laughed again, more tired than amused. "It's funny. I could have stood under a thousand swords, lived a thousand years. But you've bested me in the end."

"What happened?" Ean asked. Slowly, he lifted his hand to the branch. Part of him expected the beast to lunge; another was sure his fingers would flit through it like smoke.

But the snake didn't move and was solid when he touched it. Its skin was soft, like the hands of an elder.

"You creatures are odd," it said. "So weak, yet you hold such power. You longed for a guardian to protect the spring from the greed of others, and so I came to be. Your tales kept me strong. But there are no more tales, are there?"

Ean stared. Those who told him of the beast had passed. The children found other pursuits. Humiliation kept word of it from his own tongue.

"I expect you're the last to remember those old stories," said the beast, with a grin. "You spent all that time with your sharpened sticks when all you had to do was forget."

Ean said nothing. The beast slithered away, drifting back into the shelter of the willow tendrils. In moments it was gone, indistinguishable from the shadows of the leaves.

It was sunset by the time Ean reached the village. His wife greeted him fondly as he entered their warm cottage; his son echoed her without looking up. Ean sank silently into a chair beside the hearth, eyes fixed on a pot bubbling on the hook.

He thought victory would feel different.

His son sat cross-legged before the fire, cleaning a rifle. Ean watched for a moment as the boy's hands expertly polished and rearranged the parts into peculiar configurations.

"Boy." A mirror of his own young face, barely touched with stubble, turned toward him. Slowly, Ean folded his fingers together. "Have I ever told you of the willow beast?"

NEIGHBORHOOD RULES

Our newest case involved an amphibious being that lived in a black-water lagoon. The town had known of the lagoon since olden times: They feared its murky depths were toxic, and all were forbidden to go near it.

Regardless of its toxicity to humans, the creature itself—himself—seemed to be in good condition. His scales were clean and without any indication of rot or parasites. Most importantly, he was intellectually capable and willing to answer my questions.

"Do you consent to being recorded?" I asked the creature as I set up my equipment at the edge of the lagoon.

"Yes," replied the creature. He had a gurgling voice, like he was holding a swallow of water at the back of his throat.

"Do you confirm that consent has been given by the subject?" I asked the radio.

"Consent confirmed," crackled the voice of my supervisor, transmitted from fifty miles away.

"Let's get started," I said to the creature, who shuffled wetly out of the water to crouch across from me, his frog-like eyes unblinking and curious.

It seemed like this would be a straightforward case. The creature from the black lagoon had existed here for centuries. A wall of swamp grass served as an obvious border between his territory and the town. Unlike other creatures who suffered from humans encroaching onto their land, he only needed the lagoon itself, so being confined to the surrounding banks and a few dozen feet beyond was no great trouble. However, he was adamant that this property was his own domain.

Nothing too unusual.

We went through the questionnaire together. I marked down his answers, as his webbed hands could not manipulate a pen. The camera was set up to live stream the video to our branch office, allowing my supervisor to hear the creature's answers and check them against my transcript. Two witnesses were more trustworthy than one.

It was going smoothly enough. The creature was polite, understood me clearly, and his answers were consistent. I had reasonable hopes that this would be a straightforward inspection pass.

All went well until we reached the last question.

"Would you cause any harm to a human?"

The creature tilted his eyes down, away from me, and then back up to meet my gaze as he spoke. "On my land. I eat."

"You would eat anyone who came to your lagoon?" I repeated for the live feed. "No exceptions?"

"If my land, my prey. Grassy shore is my land. Off my land, I will not eat. On human land, I will not eat."

"Answer received?" I asked the live feed, my heart sinking.

"Received," crackled the voice of my supervisor.

"Thank you for your time," I said to the creature.

To call it the *business* of monster mediation would be inaccurate. There is very little money to be made. The creatures we work with are not abominations, but simply beings in need of advocates. I might also be biased; I may pass well as human, but am half-creature myself. (What creature, precisely, is unimportant.) That makes me the best inspector to approach rumored man-eaters. My scent is peculiar enough that they get curious rather than hungry.

"He's no ogre," I said to my supervisor, scraping mud off my boots and depositing my equipment in the supply closet. "But being willing to eat humans at all is still an issue. If only he had been more vague."

"Oh, sure," said my supervisor. "Then we'd have something much worse on our hands when some kid stumbles onto his property. Look, he's not exactly a golden case like Nessie, but at least he's upfront about his rules. If only all landowners were so frank."

"And if he breaks those rules? We'll have a riot."

My supervisor leveled an even stare at me over his glasses. "That is a concern with any neighbor. There hasn't been a casualty by the lagoon in the last fifty years, not since the town was founded, which is more than most neighbors can say. As long as he is willing to abide by the rules, I am comfortable posting a pass. Anyone living near a creature needs to accept that."

One requirement of our work: All results are available to the public within twenty-four hours after our agency passes a creature. This allows anyone living nearby to understand the needs and risks of their unique neighbors. Full transparency—that's us. No coaching, no editing.

Understandably, this can be cause for concern.

People were antsy, especially after the fishman incident in Baltimore, which is why this town reached out to us in the first place. I don't fault them; our job is to clarify rules of conduct between people and creatures to prevent such misunderstandings. In theory, if a creature can think, it can live in harmony with humans, however unusual a form that harmony took.

In theory.

I went back to the lagoon the next day and told the creature his claim would be validated, but advised he retreat anyway, as his answers might not prove acceptable to the town. I told him that our agency offered aid services, but if he wanted to be moved before our recording was made public, he needed to accept now.

He declined. They usually do.

A few months later, I got news that they ate him.

The humans didn't trespass on his territory; they caught him on theirs, around the outskirts, but not within the bounds, that had been designated as his. They riddled him with bullets and scaled him like a fish.

They were just playing by the rules he laid out, they said.

It wasn't the whole town. The incident nearly tore it apart, with clashes between those who felt their actions were justified and those who were sickened by the heinous act erupting in a riot. Still, the damage was done.

We weren't sure why he ventured out of his lagoon, until my supervisor pulled out a map of the region and pointed out a pond nearly three miles away, well beyond the creature's territory.

"There have been rumors of something living in there," he said. "Nothing substantial enough for us to get involved, but I wonder if he got lonely. Maybe he was looking for companionship."

I filed his case under "No Longer Applicable" and moved on to the next one.

It's not an uncommon ending. We like our monsters to be predictable. Not like us.

THINGS THAT GO
ᨕᨈᚦᛚᚲ
IN THE NIGHT

With a plastic *clack*, the flashlight skittered across the gravel, flinging harsh white light against the tombstones in jerky beams. A gnarled half-woman blur swept through the glare, mouth open in an earth-shaking howl.

Takeshi scrambled behind a towering gravestone, hard breaths ripping at his throat. The dusty white shape hurtled past—or he thought it did. It disappeared into the water welling in his eyes, and when he blinked there was nothing but shadows. Far away, past twisted trees and rows of cold stone, he heard Angela scream.

His phone creaked in his clutching fingers, red square blinking on its screen. Six minutes of nothing, and then . . .

The White Woman of Cherry Hill—it even *sounded* fake.

This was all supposed to be a dumb joke.

Footsteps pounded across the grass, and as Takeshi swung around something toppled over him. He screamed, trying to claw his way around the gravestone as light blasted him in the eye. Between the jumping spots that filled Takeshi's vision, Jason scrambled up from where he'd tripped, a bloody gouge on his face.

"What're you doing?" Jason screeched, snatching at the front of Takeshi's hoodie. "We have to go!"

A curtain of milky white emerged from the dark—it was a wedding dress covered in grungy lace and beads, soaked with sludge dripping from a slit throat. Liquidy black eyes pressed him to the spot. A roiling tongue stuck out of a mouth so huge it could swallow his head in one bite. It lunged forward, lips open wide, and shrieked.

Takeshi never ran faster in his life.

Delightful.

Cackling as the boys' yowls grew distant, the White Woman fluttered down onto a comfortable, flat headstone. Blessedly, it hadn't been toppled in all the fun. It wasn't as though she could sit on anything, incorporeal as she was, but the familiarity of it was nice, and she'd never be able to right it herself if some thrashing pubescent upset it.

Popping her jaw back into place, she relished the taste of their fear, like a hummingbird sipping up beads of sugar water.

In the century since her mortal form rotted away, terror never lost its sweetness—even now, when she could expect to suck the fear from dozens of gawkers each moon (all wielding shiny rectangular totems against her, their faces shimmering with strange light and images, though they were quite poor wards and they never so much as gave her a headache).

She licked her translucent fingers as the fear fluttered inside her. It made her feel more alive than she had ever been, even when she was caked in flesh.

A strange sound shivered nearby, like a handful of pebbles tossed down the path. Bending her head back, she floated through a nearby obelisk and squinted down the rows. She was sure only four ne'er-do-wells had entered the cemetery this evening, and all four had presently retreated. Had she missed one? She rose into the air, unleashing a howl that made the grass quiver. But there was nothing there, and no echo of the tinkling sound remained in its wake.

What was left of her eyebrow climbed delicately up her forehead. Strange. She had resided in this graveyard for hundreds of years, knew its every branch and creaking gate, and never had she heard a sound like that before.

Something gurgled. With a wispy pop, her head snapped around, yet she found nothing waiting down the dark path. A twist of unease in her belly, she slowly drifted back toward her favorite monument—one with a great stone door that insulated her from the wind. Quite the annoyance, this was, but surely it was nothing.

But as she flitted across the yard, her bare toes wafting through the dewdrops and earth, she realized she felt cold, her body misting as it shivered. But that wasn't possible. She couldn't feel cold—she couldn't feel anything at all.

She jerked when the tinkling began again, louder this time. Stretching her mouth wide, she filled the yard with a gutteral shriek. But nothing stumbled out of the dark—or no *one*. At the shallow edge of the shadows, brushed by moonlight, she saw the stones ripple like water in a pond. Deep within, something moved, far beyond her sight. She felt it, knew it was there—that it was looking back at her.

The chill rushed through her arms and legs and set in her chest like a rock. Without a thought she bolted toward the monument. Surely she'd be safe there, within a home meant to guard the dead! But something slithered through her ankle, and then she couldn't move. It pulled her tight. With a shrill gasp she tried to fly away, but had long forgotten how to yank free of anything.

Her eyes flicked to the ground below, and she half felt, half saw a gaping maw pulling her in.

For the first time in hundreds of years, her scream was real.

DEEP DOWN

As I turn to the first weathered page of your journal, I look out upon your watery grave: an endless, dark, and chilling sea. It and this logbook are all I have left of you. I hope that the image I see when I look at my reflection is what you carried with you on your expedition. I hope that you recalled holding me close the day before you left, both of us staring at ourselves in the mirror of the vanity you gave me on our wedding day. But I fear your journal will tell me something much different.

You decided to go alone. You wouldn't tell your team why. That was just like you: closed off like an impenetrable vault, mind full of precious knowledge. I cried and begged you to stay. Reminded you that you swore never to leave. You promised it would be a short expedition and that you'd be back soon.

There were others who could have taken your place on that routine journey beneath the waves. But I knew the truth: Disease had struck me, and you couldn't bear to lay eyes on my withering body. Our thirty years together seemed to matter little to you.

Within your submersible, you did everything you could to keep from thinking of me. You spent many late nights researching and documenting nautical discoveries in peace. Then, in September 1963—your second month alone—you noted disturbing anomalies: distant cries that echoed from the deep, and strange radio signals. You looked for answers in the murky distance, peering from your porthole windows, but your reflection made you feel uneasy.

You swore you were not alone. The sounds you once heard from the gloomy depths now came from within your submarine. Noises from creaking pipes became anguished laments. Your frantic scribbling on October 6th said you searched every inch of your vessel for an intruder, but found nothing. Meanwhile, the voices grew louder.

Your reflection in the portholes provided your only sense of reality and safety, however fleeting. But that wasn't all you saw. On October 8th, your stalker finally emerged. Its guise was familiar even as the sight of it through the porthole clawed at your soul. It would pass here and there, always right behind you as you struggled to stare only at yourself. You would call out, begging it to leave you be, but it only came closer. You tried to avoid the porthole, but without it, despair crept on even faster.

It tore at your mind over many sleepless nights. The misshapen visage called for you, begging you to look it in the eye, but you refused. Your last entry on October 19th reveals you had not slept for ten days and couldn't keep anything down. Your body was failing. With your last ounce of strength, you fumbled with the controls to return to the surface. But you refused to open your eyes to use them.

All these years later, we still cannot make sense of what you saw or heard. They recovered your vessel with your shriveled body inside, your hands gripping your journal; it found its way to me, but your team insisted I never open its pages. Now I wish I hadn't.

As I reach the end, something jumps to my attention. Among its final, blank pages, I find a photo of us in front of the vanity, taken the day we were told I had only weeks to live. There is no warmth in your smile, only fear, despair, and hopelessness.

After all these years, I can hardly recognize myself beneath the bandages. Instead, I see your monster—your guilt. I recovered, but you'll never know. You'll never know that I fought because of you, even while you ran.

LIKE FATHER

"Is the doctor in tonight?" Stein calls, knocking on the closed door. No one answers. He glances around, taking in various stimuli and data points. Streetlamps fizzle in and out. Fresh puddles reflect dingy buildings. Rats scurry around corners. The air is wet and smells like sewage. It is a far cry from the warmth of home.

Stein's data scan flashes in his periphery and confirms he's in the right location. Pulling the collar of his long black coat tighter around his face, he turns down an adjacent alley and spots a slime-crusted window. It shatters easily under his immense fist, and his towering body cracks the wooden frame as he squeezes through the broken glass. The room is completely black.

"Father."

The voice startles Stein as he squints into the darkness. He considers activating his night vision, but hesitates. Perhaps the dark will make the conversation easier.

"Why have you come?" the voice asks. "You could have let three years become twenty, then eternity." Stein is unable to respond; hearing Junior's metallic voice jumbles the code in his processor core. The quiet whirring of Stein's hardware is all that can be heard. His son scoffs, "What, no long soliloquies about the terrible choices I've made?"

Stein runs through several scenarios he previously rehearsed and finally settles on the most promising one. "It's time you came home, Junior."

His son lets out a sharp laugh that sounds of steel grates clanking on iron chains. Stein winces.

"You don't sound well, Junior. You must come home. I know things were not . . . the best when you left, but it isn't safe for our kind here."

"Not safe?" More creaking laughter. "How was it any safer to lock your 'magnum opus' away?"

"You weren't ready to face the world yet. I was only trying to . . . "

"Yes, yes, the grandest cliche every parent tells their child. You wanted to shield me from the world, from disapproving eyes and pitchforks."

Stein shakes his head at the dark shadow across the room. "I wanted to protect you by perfecting you, to let you walk in the world knowing you are a god among mortals."

A chair scrapes the cement floor as Junior bellows, "How can I be a model of perfection when I'm made of the innocents you *murdered?*"

"Because you were to be the best of them in every way!"

Neon lights blare to life, blinding Stein. As his eyes adjust, he gasps at the sight before him.

"No. What have you done?"

Junior glares back, face torn in half. A piece of skin droops over the boy's metal cheek, flapping in time with his breathing. Glints of silver flash beneath red scalp tissue. The other half of his face is intact—a perfect cream complexion with one stormy blue eye peering from underneath a mop of black curls.

"Don't like what you see, Father?" Junior asks with clenched fists. Like his mutilated visage, one arm has been stripped of skin and meat—bone and metal and wire are visible for all to see. Stein stares, horrified. "Neither do I. All I can see in the mirror are the men you've torn apart to create me."

"Foolish child," Stein says. He can feel the cylinders and pistons within him firing faster, blood and oil rushing through his body as thought processes flit through his brain. "How dare you destroy yourself to spite me," he roars.

"Spite?" Junior spits. "Are you really so blind? Can you not see you've become the very man you despise?"

In three strides, Stein crosses the room and grabs Junior by the throat, pushing him against the wall. Remnants of delicate stitches peek out at him—a reminder of his painstaking work blending skin tones and hiding blemishes. It is a stark contrast to his own yellowed complexion and coal black lips. How could his son strip it all away?

He squeezes a fraction tighter. Junior clutches Stein's mottled arm and pants, "Like father, like son."

Stein immediately releases him and steps back, staring at his own shaking hands, each the size of a rotting bear paw. Falling to his knees and covering his face, he whispers, "I am not my father."

Junior heaves and rubs his throat. Finally, the boy stands tall and gleaming under the hazy lights, a dark glare fixed on Stein.

"And I'm not you, Father," Junior says. "I do not claim to be more or less than what I am, nor do I expect the world to be cruel or kind. I know it to be both, and I will meet it either way." Without another word, he strides toward the door.

His words hit Stein like lightning. They convey the very thing he wished his maker had taught him. But instead he was forced to scrounge through weathered books, searching for comfort in the philosophies of dead men. A mixture of pride and sorrow colors his reply.

"My choices made you who you are, therefore I regret nothing," Stein murmurs. Junior pauses at the door. "I hope you can forgive me, one day."

The hinges creak; a rush of cool air blows in and Stein is left alone, staring at the empty room before him.

LUCA THE GREAT

The limbs of autumn trees swayed over the savior of Florence like the arms of a welcoming crowd. The young hero followed the cobblestone road atop his mighty war horse, grinning widely at the coin in his hand. Against the setting sun, the face on the gilded piece glinted nearly as bright as the hero's pearl-white teeth.

"The bards will be singing of this day for years to come," the young man chuckled. Flipping open the visor of his burgonet, he wiped sweat from a handsome, chiseled face and glanced behind him. "Wouldn't you say, old Piero?"

More bone than animal, the donkey Piero snorted, hobbling beneath the bags of gold tied to his thin form. His master took the animal's feeble grunt as sincere agreement.

"Of course, they will! I already know what I'll tell them. How I, Luca the Great, braved the perils of the centaur's forest. Oh, the riches he guarded! They'll tell of the unimaginable wealth Luca the Great took from the beast that only he was brave enough to face." Luca hopped down from his horse with his halberd in hand, slashing and stabbing theatrically at the air.

"They'll sing of how I charged into his glade without fear. How I cursed him for preying on young Florentine women for all these years and warned him of his impending death! The centaur let loose countless arrows, but I, swift and strong, caught them in mid-flight with my bare hands. Then, I vanquished the beast with a single mighty blow." He paused, looking to the blade of his perfectly polished halberd.

"Ah, the might of the centaur's hooves, heavy as anvils, and his torso and arms thick as a Titan's! The legends of his foulness will nearly match those of my glory, Piero. I shall become a figure of myth like the goddess Minerva herself! I truly am the savior of Florence. . . ." He opened his mouth to continue his boast, but instead squinted at Piero.

"Well, donkey, you get the point." He pulled a handkerchief from within his breastplate, wiping dust from the arm of his intricate and pristine plate armor. "This tale is better told to a more appreciative audience."

Luca mounted his war horse and continued on, his donkey hardly able to keep pace, until a distant rustling disturbed the quiet. He looked up the road to see a ragged figure emerge from the burnt reds and oranges of the tree line.

"That's far enough, mighty hero," the figure said.

Luca eyed the man's frayed dress and rusty sword. "Out of my way, peasant. I'm returning from a great quest and can't be bothered by your ilk. Run along now. Go back to whatever hole you crawled out from."

The man came closer. "I don't think so. I'll be taking that gold you've got there. The families of the centaur's victims are more deserving of these riches than you."

"Brigand! Do you know who I am?" Luca laughed, fidgeting with the reins.

"I know quite well. I've been following you for many days now, Luca, 'savior of Florence.'"

Luca glared. "All right now, thief, you've had your fun." He flipped his visor closed, hopped down from his horse with a loud clanking of steel, and pointed his halberd at the man. "This is your final warning. Be gone or face my wrath!"

Instead of stepping aside, the stranger pulled a sack from his belt and tossed it to the ground. It landed with a thud, and the centaur's bloodied head rolled out.

Luca leapt back in horror. "How did you . . .?"

The man stepped closer. "My daughter was killed by this beast. I set out from Florence two days ago to seek a father's revenge, only to find you had reached the centaur first. Though not for the reasons you boasted." He looked over Luca's spotless armor. "I see that the fabled Luca the Great was not as iron-willed as they say, and instead of ridding the people of this menace, traded his once-legendary strength for the promise of riches."

"Silence! That curse is but a fable . . . and I did nothing of the sort!" Luca charged forward without warning. But when his weapon met the stranger's sword, the man's parry sent the halberd flying and Luca crashing to the ground in a heap of metal. He tried to lift himself, but fumbled beneath the weight of his armor.

"How? What is this? I feel so weak," he whimpered.

"You are forever cursed now, undone by your own greed. You have been deceived, and now with the centaur dead you won't receive the endless riches he promised. But you'll still pay his price, and you'll linger in this world, sapped of all your strength."

The man suddenly reached for his belt, making Luca flinch. Instead of a weapon, he pulled an apple from his pouch. He held the fruit out to Piero, and as the donkey munched away, the man untied the bags of gold from the animal's saddle. They dropped to the ground. Luca watched, eyes wide.

"Well, hero, we'd better get going," the man said, as he mounted the war horse. "We've got a long way to go before nightfall, and you've a lot of gold to carry."

SIREN SONG

The people of Willhaven Port rose to the bells of the salt-beaten church each dawn, called to waiting nets and hungry crab pots. But today they were roused by Corrina's shriek clawing through the soupy fog.

They found her on the shore, hunched in the waves' frothy path. Tomas' blood was wet on her frock; he lay limp in her arms as the townsfolk gathered around them, a cocoon of gasps and murmurs.

Her wail sharpened when they pulled his body away, but by then she was spent, falling into Mrs. Baker's arms. They laid him across the sand, his sightless eyes staring up at the sky. Angry gashes shredded him from collarbone to hip, turning his belly to a nest of gore.

"What happened, child?" barked the butcher. Corrina seemed not to hear him. She wept softly against Mrs. Baker's chest, wrapping her arms around her own round stomach.

He grumbled, but no others had the heart to push her. The only surviving kin of their late fleet-owning father, the brother and sister were all each other had, even after Corrina married this past spring. They were a kind and noble set, and Tomas, a steadfast dockmaster—to see this befall them, of all people, was horror enough itself.

When Corrina did speak, it was to no one. "Monster," she bleated, her arm stretching toward the water. It was only then that they saw the bloody slice in Corrina's shoulder.

"Wake the doctor!" Mrs. Baker yelled.

"Monster," Corrina cried, her voice growing louder. "*Monster!* It came—it came and, and it—"

She fell back into her wordless wail. The townsfolk stiffened as one and turned toward the familiar waters, wreathed in mist.

As Corrina sat in the Bakers' oven-warmed kitchen, hands wrapped around a cup of barley tea, the story drifted out of her.

They had been walking on the beach, she said. Her husband was gone on a fortnight's trawl, as he often was, and she was happy for her brother's company. They had just left the shipyard behind in the mist when Tomas spotted a shadow darting through the surf toward them. He was drawing the gutting knife from his hip when the creature reached the shore and lunged.

"It was woman at the top but fish from the belly down," she stammered, fingers curled tight around the mug. "It had gray skin like stone, all covered in scales. It attacked us."

She forced back a sob. Mrs. Baker squeezed her hand kindly. "Blessedly be that you and the baby are safe."

The assembled townsfolk, packed into the kitchen like sardines, were taken with a different thought. A murmur swept through the crowd. None wanted to believe in something out of those old sailors' tales, but her words left little doubt.

"What then, child?" said the old blacksmith.

Even as Mrs. Baker glared at him, Corrina shook her head and answered. "He must've cut it bad, because it screamed and fell back in the water. I thought he'd saved us both. But then—he dropped the knife in the water and—"

That was enough. Sobs overtook her, and Mrs. Baker ushered everyone out with a wave of a brawny arm. As the entire town of Willhaven shuffled into the street, one whisper drifted between them: *"Siren."*

Ellair hummed as she skipped along the creaking wooden walkway. Corrina followed several paces behind, enjoying the cool air on her skin. Her daughter was full of boundless energy and only seemed to gather more by the day, while it was a struggle for Corrina to hold onto any of hers.

But this, at least, they both enjoyed: walking the path that ran along the shoreline. The town built it in the wake of her brother's death, far enough from the surf to avoid grasping claws, and it was only now starting to show the wear of salt and sand.

"Which way is the sun, dove?" Corrina asked through her fatigue, looking off to the horizon. Ellair's father had given her a small gold compass as a gift, which clacked as the girl held it in her swinging hand.

"East!" the girl said triumphantly, pointing toward a bloom of pale light where the sun was starting to rise.

Corrina sighed and looked out toward the surf as Ellair scuttled ahead. The path wasn't the same as a proper walk in the sand. But it had been five years, and the town had begun to calm once more. Perhaps one day, she could tread the beach and feel the waves wash over her feet without a sidelong glance . . .

Her steps slowed as she peered into the fading fog. Stones peppered the outer shoreline, buffered against the greatest of the waves. But one was strangely shaped, far taller than the rest.

On the rock, its fin slapping lazily against the water, perched a siren.

Corrina stopped. Woman above and fish below, its claws were thin but short, and no needle teeth jutted from its mouth. And yet, it could be nothing else.

It wasn't possible.

Blinking hard, she tried to wash it from her sight. It was just a specter! But when she opened her eyes again, the siren was still there, running thin fingers through the ends of its kelpy hair. It made no move to swim closer, but its gaze alone pierced into her like one of its claws.

You blamed me, it seemed to say.

It couldn't be here. It wasn't real. But as she stared and it stayed stubbornly fleshy, the thoughts tumbled into her mind unbidden. *It wasn't my fault.*

Her brother found out the truth about the baby, about the other man. He was furious, disgusted she would sully the family name—that much she expected after he signed her away with all the care he gave to his ships' catch. But then he demanded her share of their father's inheritance and more. He swore to reveal her if she parted with any less, and she'd known the bastard long enough to be sure he would keep his word. He would have ruined her.

More delicately than its putrid shape seemed able, it reached one long arm behind itself and plucked something from the rock. A gutting knife.

Corrina's heart tumbled into her stomach. She could feel the hilt in her hand as if she had just flung it into the sea. Turning the blade deftly, the siren pointed it at her.

No. Behind her.

"Mumma?"

Corrina jumped at the sound, whirling like a frightened animal. Ellair stepped back, the compass clutched in her hands. Corrina stammered, eyes flying back to the water, and found nothing but stones caught in the foam.

"What's wrong?" Ellair said, a sniffle in her voice.

Corrina took a painfully long moment to answer. "Nothing," she choked out. "Nothing, my dove. Let's go home."

She took Ellair by the hand and held tight as she turned them back down the path, waves crashing loud in her ears. The weight in her palm would not fade away.

ABOMINABLE

"Quickly," Ehani whispered, motioning for me to crouch beside her. "Over there." I squinted and tried to see why she was so excited. But there were only snow-covered boulders against the side of the mountain crags.

"What are you—?" I said, but stopped an instant later, words frozen in my throat. Not a hundred feet away, the boulders began shuffling down a narrow cliff path, and what I thought was snow became shaggy piles of ice-crusted fur.

Ehani chuckled and kissed my cheek, snapping me out of my stupor. I tore the cap off my telephoto lens and took a flurry of shots. With each *click*, I sputtered out question after question: "How did you know they would be here? Could we get closer to tag one? Have your people been hiding them?"

Ehani stayed silent. I didn't notice. In between shots, I was jotting down notes, frantic to remember every detail.

"You said you were here for snow leopards," she finally whispered, pointing at my notebook. "What is this, Lynnea?"

"It's nothing," I said, moving away. "I'm a scientist first; you know that. This is huge! It'll change the world."

As I continued zooming in, collecting vital evidence, Ehani snatched the book from my hands.

"Hey!" I yelled, trying to grab it back. But she was already clambering down the ledge, away from the lookout. By the time I reached her, she had flipped to the earlier entries, engrossed in what she found.

"It's not what you think," I said. "I was going to tell you."

Ignoring my shouting, she started reading aloud: "The *metch-kangmi* has never been closer. 'The creature that is neither man nor beast' must be one of the village's charges. Ehani is hiding it from me; I know it. And if I'm wrong, I know the nomadic village's routes and how often they move to follow and protect the creatures. Ehani has told me plenty about this harsh land— enough to survive alone. One way or another, I will find it. I'll do whatever it takes to make the world believe me."

She paused and, without looking up, asked, "Will you?"

I turned away, unsure how to reply. I had planned to tell her sooner, but days became weeks and weeks grew into months where the lies remained hidden under layers of laughter and stories of our childhoods. She had finally introduced me to her village, then her family. Despite their wariness, her fervent arguments about my good intentions eventually swayed their minds. The guilt lay heavy within my heart as I found myself falling for her. I kept repeating, *Today the lies end*, but I couldn't bring myself to do it.

Each hike was longer than the last, leading to more moments under the stars. I followed her people through beautiful valleys and mountains, learning they were devout protectors of the land and its creatures. The delight on Ehani's face as she taught me their ways made me think of the truth less and less.

"Seventeen years," I finally said, "proving this thing exists is my life's work. Do you know what it's like to be laughed at for something you believe in with every atom of your being?"

Ehani stared at me then, her dark brown eyes tinged with tears. "Yes. I spoke for you when my people wanted you to leave, when they said you were just some Western woman here to expose us. I fought for you."

Like a fish on land, my mouth opened and closed, sputtering with indecision as I struggled to find the words back to her.

A roar sounded in the distance, tearing my attention from her face; the yeti seemed to be communicating through intense grunts and bellows.

Ehani sighed and threw the notebook at my feet. "Wait," I said to her. She did not slow her pace. But the yeti paused their trek, and I could not help but stay to observe a bit longer—mesmerized by the care and attention each paid to the other.

The snow had already buried her footsteps by the time I looked back.

Now, the snow was falling faster and the wind's icy claws crept into my heavy fur parka. A blizzard was brewing on the horizon.

Without an experienced guide, two hours in a storm could easily become three or more. All traces of the village would vanish, as if they never existed, and with them, Ehani. Any chance at begging for forgiveness would disappear.

I shed the weight of my camera bag and research equipment. There was already so little time, and I had made my choice.

A BABYSITTER'S DUTY

It was the only time I ever took a referral.

Most of the families I babysat for are all on the same grape-vine of streets in our town. Professor Smythe, however, had rented a very nice house about a fifteen-minute drive away. It belonged to the university—no one remembered who the original owner was, but the others who previously lodged there never stayed for long, so it had been empty for some time.

Professor Smythe was an anthropology professor, all about liminality, which was not surprising. Because that house, on its own in the fields, surrounded by a small grove of trees? That was fucking liminality defined. My car started shuddering the second I pulled off the road onto the long dirt driveway that led up to the house.

Inside, the place was lovely—every surface was lined with paintings and masks and other decorative items that distinguished professors get to collect. I was told most of it had come with the place.

Professor Smythe and his wife were deeply grateful to see me. They'd been dying to get out of the house, they said. It had been feeling a little too cramped for their tastes, but their son, Grayson, didn't want to be left alone. Should have been my first clue.

The second clue was how nervous the boy looked when his parents walked out the door. I wasn't worried at the time—kids could be totally fine until the moment the person they trust is no longer in view.

"Want to watch?" I asked, gesturing to the very nice TV mounted in the corner. An hour of TV before bed couldn't hurt. I'd have to make sure I didn't fall asleep myself, maybe find the thermostat to turn down the heat.

He shook his head. "Can we play doctor?"

I raised an eyebrow at him, purposefully exaggerating my skepticism. Kids seemed to like it when I proved I could contort my face like in the best of their cartoons. "Depends. What kind of checkup am I getting?"

"A normal one," the kid said evasively, shifting from foot to foot. "Can I get my kit?"

"Sure," I said, and he ran to his room, footsteps barely making any sound on the plush rug. I took a seat on the squashy leather sofa. Like everything else in the house, it was surprisingly warm. By the time he came back—and he wasn't gone very long—I was half-dozing off.

It went all right at first; just the usual "tests." Thankfully, he wasn't nearly as enthusiastic using that little hammer on my knees as other brats I've dealt with.

"Okay, now I need your blood," said Grayson, pulling out a very real syringe.

As fast as I could, I was out of my seat and on the other side of the coffee table.

"Where the *fuck* did you get that?"

Broke rule one: Don't swear around the kids.

Not that it mattered at the moment.

He looked dead serious. "I need some blood."

"Grayson, that's dangerous; put it down." I came back around the table, reaching for his hand to take the syringe away.

He tried to stab me.

"Hey, hey!"

"Hold still!"

Dodging another stab attempt, I desperately looked around the room for a way to take away the syringe. I jumped over the coffee table and realized that I'd made three entire circuits of the room in this little chase. Not that it was a big room, but it suddenly felt even smaller, as if I could stretch both arms and touch the opposing walls, like some weird optical illusion.

"You need to hold still!" yelled Grayson, stamping his foot.

"Grayson, no games with blood, okay? I don't know what your parents let you—"

"My parents don't know!" Grayson's eyes were wide, and he was trembling. "He and Mom got the house without learning about it. If you want to get out, you need to give it blood!"

Okay. Haven't heard that one before.

He was clearly panicking, darting back and forth like a football player doing a shuffle, trying to predict my next move.

Smart kid, but I had longer legs; it wasn't hard for me to dodge out of the way.

Grayson took a deep breath and . . . promptly ran away.

I gave myself a moment to catch my breath, then went after him.

My head almost brushed the ceiling in the hallway to the bedrooms, though I could have sworn there had been more room when I first came in. And even here the hall was so narrow, I had to turn sideways to move through it. Was it just me or was it hotter, too? Maybe because I hadn't turned down the temperature.

Or maybe it was something else.

A closed door. If there was anywhere he would hide, it would probably be behind a bedroom door. I shimmied up to it, yanked it open, and ran inside. No Grayson, but I quickly let go of the burning doorknob under my palm.

"Why did you go in there?"

I turned and saw Grayson just outside the door frame, still clutching the syringe, even more terrified than before.

"I've been trying to keep it happy!" he wailed. "Blood works sometimes, but then it got the dog, and now I don't know what will happen!"

"What?"

"The house! It came with all of this stuff—it all belonged to the people before who didn't leave! They got eaten instead!" He was shrinking into himself, like he wanted to curl up into a ball and hide. He stared pleadingly at me. "It's getting closer; can't you feel it?"

I could. The walls were bending as if all the air in the room was being sucked out, pressing closer.

The babysitter is supposed to keep their kid safe, right? Well, that's what I would do.

I grabbed Grayson, dragging him by the hand right as his room dissolved completely into blackness.

We reached the front door, which was still just barely big enough for him to fit through, but far too small for me. I ignored the scorching handle and pushed him out, slamming the door shut so it wouldn't suck him back in. As the floor and walls pulled together, I could hear his scream in the distance.

Poor Grayson.

By the time the house had finished digesting me (if that's the best word), I don't think even blood would have stopped it from trying to get his family. Now, at least, I'd bought him some time.

Because he wasn't wrong: I disappeared last night, but I didn't go anywhere.

I'm still here, between the leftmost arm of the couch and the elegant mask-set against the wall—all things the previous owners brought, all with their own secrets.

You'll find me in the wallpaper.

THE DRAGON COMETH

"Any sign of the train?" Eleanor's father asked, straightening under the bright sun. He repeated that question every hour, without fail.

"Not yet," replied Eleanor, without looking up from the ground where she knelt. It was summer and the earth was dry and cracked and flat where the teeth of the railroad chomped steadily towards them. They would hear the train well before they saw it.

"It'll be good for your mother to finally meet your grandfather now that we have him settled, even if it is only in spirit," Eleanor's father said as he knelt beside her. The two of them glanced at her grandfather's gravestone, set firmly in its place of honor in their new, sparse cemetery. It had cost a pretty penny, and the engraver needed instructions to spell her grandfather's name right. But they had it now, and that was the important part. Her father knew the path to the accident site, and together they would extract Grandfather's bones. They would finally give him a proper burial, not far from the very tracks he and the other Chinese workers helped lay.

Eleanor felt it was morbid, but her father was firm in his conviction that it would have been Grandfather's wish. She would honor that.

"Would he have liked her?" she asked. "If they could have met in life?"

"I don't know," said her father after a pause. "I think he always hoped to bring over a girl from our village for me, but I found your mother first."

"How should I address him again?" she asked.

"Yéye," he replied.

Grandfather—*"Yéye,"* she practiced in her head—deserved a true resting place. This town was young; coming to an agreement with the townsfolk on setting up a cemetery was less of a struggle than it could have been. This little plot would stand for the railroad workers who were buried in the avalanche all those years ago. Not too close to the town's proper cemetery, of course, but as long as their family did their business and moved on, the townspeople would mind theirs in turn.

And it would not be just Grandfather. There were other bones lost in the mountains, belonging to other men the train had eaten. It would be right to give them a resting place as well.

"Just in case their families come looking for them one day," said Eleanor's father.

He straightened again, peering out to the west. "Do you hear that?"

The roar was faint and preceded by a small stream of smoke drifting up from the horizon. Eleanor stiffened, turning to watch.

It was coming.

She could picture it now: its shiny black skin and glowing golden eye, the silvery metal bars that made up its teeth, its steady tread forward. The thing that killed her grandfather and others like him so it could exist, demanding sacrifices of sweat and blood and bone. It was like the creatures from her mother's stories—greedy beasts that needed to be subdued by saints.

Yet, its length and the way it twined through the landscape reminded Eleanor of her father's stories. She thought of those benevolent creatures with long, shimmering bodies that twisted and twined, whose likenesses danced through the streets of San Francisco. And this creature of fire and old, blackened wood, cruel as its birth was, would bring her mother and sister to them so they could honor Grandfather as a family.

The train would draw all eyes towards it, a familiar mark on the landscape, yet still so new. The people of the town would come and watch as the packages they relied on for survival were carried from the train, followed by alien passengers.

Soon they would see a fierce Teutonic woman—square-jawed, short, and beautiful—step onto the platform as confidently as if she was born there. They would see her young compan-

58

ion follow her like a duckling. But they would be confused by the epicanthic fold above the girl's light brown eyes and her broad, rounded cheekbones. An incomplete picture of a family— they would see more when Eleanor and her father arrived at the station.

The train roared again, louder this time.

"How far away do you think it is?" he asked her.

"Not far," said Eleanor.

"Let's get back to town."

The metal monster was coming. Despite breaking the last generation apart, it would now bring this one together.

THE SPIDER JAR

I put myself in this jar. It was left open and exposed to the elements, so why not take it as my own?

Others might think it a prison, but it is a satisfying home for me. I only have these spindly limbs and the silk from my own body. So, what does one do when all they have is time and raw material?

Make something.

Athena, you bitch. You were cruel, but you knew what you were doing. Humans scatter, at best, when they see me. Or they lunge after me, which makes it important to find places to hide.

What beautiful work, they cry, *but what a disgusting little creature that made it.*

Still, I endure.

I spin with far more deftness and delicacy in this form than I ever did before. And when my energy is spent, I consume my own silk for sustenance, which is more than I could make of my art when I was human.

Now, being stuck like this and with the act of creation so easy, my mind drifts. Oh, Muse, will the story of my life after my transformation ever be told? Will they sing of how Arachne whiled away her days, not at the mercy of a goddess, but by her own desire?

No, they will say, *not unless you can find a way to repent and become a woman again.*

I think not.

This form is not as comely, but I create better this way.

Athena, you bitch, you still see the beauty in my work, even when you disagree with my subjects. I know the stories of Zeus well; that I don't see his seductions as anything but a series of tragedies is simply a matter of perspective. That I made them my subject is the artist's prerogative.

Perhaps this transformation was truly meant to be a gift. The gods have worked in stranger ways. Athena's work has its own grace, but mine is still equal in skill to hers, and it has greater use now. It is my home, and it is how I earn my dinner. How many artists can say that their work feeds them as mine does? It is worthy of a little pride.

It is easy to spin in this jar. A limited space is more than enough to work with. The gods do not understand how our limitations push us to create finer and finer work—they who have everything. Athena still does not understand what made my work exceed hers, she who is touched with gifts beyond my mean understanding.

There is a scraping from above. Has Athena come to see what I've created in the dark?

No, it's just a fleshy human face that peers in, and one that screams. The jar falls and rolls. It's a miracle that it doesn't break, but now my beautiful threads have been torn and ruined and I must begin again. For that alone, I would have bitten the human if she had come near enough.

Linen does not do this; truly, I miss it sometimes. I miss making art for others that can be used again and again, rather than for myself.

Time to find somewhere else. I scuttle away. I need a dark corner, somewhere undisturbed, so I can keep creating. Did Athena think this would be part of the curse, that my work would endure if no human sees it? That I can only make it in places of dust and neglect?

Nonsense. I will live for it, for what I can create.

My victims know that I am an artist. My art is what catches them unawares, lulls them with its beauty, makes a permanent mark on their consciousness.

And one day soon, the web that brings my dinner will hold my children.

Here's a new container, hidden in the back of this dwelling. I see cobwebs from other artists long dead. Excellent. A perfect site to begin a new work.

The best art comes from monsters—everyone knows that.

Now, was I monstrous before I was transformed by an act of jealousy?

I have you, Athena, to thank for that, for I didn't start that way. I just happened to be one of the unfortunate girls that made you angry. But that's all right. There are hundreds of us, and there will be hundreds more. More than you can count. And we shall keep spinning, for that is our purpose. It is what we live for.

HONEY AND DATES

On their third date, Mary makes a terrible mistake: she touches his hand.

They are strolling through streets of Halloween trimmings and colorful costumes. At her side, Derrick nods through a sea of masks to a man dressed as a ghost with a bottle of beer in each hand. "He's about to get sheet-faced."

It is a horrible joke. She cackles all the same, mirth and something even lighter bubbling in her chest as her fingers brush over his knuckles. But her smile falters when he turns to her and his eyes widen, gaze darting over her face and body.

Dread plummets into her stomach like a stone. She jerks away, frantically inspecting her gloved hands. A gasp tumbles over her lip when she sees the hole in the crease of her thumb.

"I am sorry," she blurts. Derrick peers at her, green eyes sharp as spears. "I—there is somewhere I have to be."

She does not wait for an answer. She vanishes into the crowd, tears welling in her eyes.

Her glamour can fool even the most discerning gaze. But a touch passes through it.

The next night, as Mary stares at her honey-coated fingers, a knock comes at the door. She starts—her small apartment never sees visitors.

"Mary," Derrick's silvery voice filters through. "Can we talk? Please?"

Slowly, she rises, setting down her bowl of honeyed dates. A dozen half-formed thoughts buzz through her head like locusts. But something goads her, taking root in her chest, and she unlocks the door with a faint click.

Derrick stands on her doorstep, smiling almost apologetically. He lifts a cloth grocery bag as if presenting a peace offering. The neck of a bottle catches the white of the streetlights. "I brought the good stuff."

Mary's eyes flit from the bag to his smile. She moves from the door as if in a fog. Soon she is perched on her futon, watching as he twists a corkscrew into a bottle of mead.

His face is pale behind curly black hair, but his green eyes twinkle with life—just as they did when she first saw his photo, grinning up at her from her phone. She hesitated then. (There

was little point; whatever came of this was doomed to failure.)
But that strange, starving thing inside her forced her hand, and
she sent his countenance to the east with a flick.

They met for a hot drink not long after. She learned they
liked the same music, and neither could wait for the next episode of *A Royal Game*. They talked with equal passion about
the environment, ancient history, and their love of cats. He had a
kindness about his smile.

"So," he says, handing her a tumbler of gold liquid.

She expects him to ask why she ran. He has the gentle eyes
for it, and it would explain his calm demeanor. She wonders if
luck has been exceptionally kind. Perhaps he never saw through
her glamour at all.

"How does a lovely mummy like you end up in Austin, of all
places?"

In that moment, her apartment was quieter than the grave.
When the archaeologist read the scroll of life and beauty that was
buried beside her, Mary heard the sighing of stones and skitter-
ing of insects. When her sarcophagus was flown across the sea,
she heard the bustling of the scientists as if in a dream. But now,
as she clutches her drink and stares at Derrick's smirk, silence
presses in around them like earth.

"What sort of question is that?" she says evenly, but she
knows it is a weak charade. There is no denying what he saw
with his own eyes.

"Yeah, I guess it's hot here," he says, comically rubbing his
chin. "And the Colorado's a bit like the Nile . . ."

Her lips press into a thin line as the plastic strains under her fingers. "Are you here to mock me?"

The mirth falls from his mouth. "No, that's not—"

"If not that, then what? Am I some curiosity? Or perhaps you think to sell me to the highest bidder?" Her voice rises as she slams the glass down on her coffee table. He may know the truth beneath her magic concealment, but she will not tolerate whatever sick plot drew him here after. "I will have you know, mortal, that the curses of my ancestors will make you regret—"

He bares his teeth. Two knife-sharp incisors grow and stretch to the edge of his lower lip. Her words turn to dust in her mouth.

"You . . ." she starts as he collects her glass and refills it.

"Hey, I asked you first," he says, offering her the drink. "How does a mummy end up in Austin?"

She does not take it. Her fingers rise to her cheek, dragging lines down her skin. Beneath, she feels the ancient bandages and brittle grooves of her true face. Her eyes mist.

"Hey," he says, his voice and eyes suddenly softer. "All right, I'll go first. I came to the New World in the 1600s and set up as a fur trader in Quebec. Had the good fortune to get bitten by some bald, naked thing in the woods. Woke up with the thirst and haven't stayed put for the last four-hundred years." Shifting closer, he holds out the drink again. "Didn't have to change my name, though. I'm guessing that's not the case for you."

"Why are you doing this?" she sniffs, glancing at his quirked eyebrow and the charming curve of his chin. Just looking at him makes her chest ache. "I do not need your pity."

68

"What? No! This is amazing! I want to know everything about you."

"I . . ." She does not wish to say it. She has spent a decade hiding, never uttering a word. "I am not alive. I do not even have blood! What could you want from me?"

Derrick's eyes are still shining. "Do you know how many times I've swiped right on someone who ends up having some weird blood kink? Too many. It's like they're fetishizing you, you know?"

"I do not."

"Well, it sucks. Pun intended."

She cannot help it: she snorts, and loudly.

"And you like my stupid jokes! Look, seriously, this is amazing. I want to get to know you better. I mean it."

He takes her bare hand before she can pull back. She nearly jerks away, feeling his cool skin against the gaps in her flesh. But he drifts over the impressions, weaving their fingers together. Slowly, like sand being tugged by the tide, she relaxes.

"So?" He pulls at the word, his voice tinged with hope.

She lets out a breath. "I am Meryt-Heqet," she stammers for the first time in this life, and accepts the cup. "I escaped from the Los Angeles Natural History Museum ten years ago."

"That was *you?*" he gapes, fingers tightening around hers. "Holy shit, I have to hear this."

HYPERBOREAN

I first grew suspicious of Dr. Khatris when he started locking himself in his lab every night. I hadn't slept in days; when I began to suspect the bastard was scheming against me, I threw my work aside. He thinks I didn't see him sneaking in from the blizzard three nights ago. But I saw enough. The moment the son of a bitch came into the cargo bay hauling that frozen lifeless mass behind his snowmobile, everything changed.

He thinks I suspect nothing, that I didn't hear him radio Expanse Medical, declaring that the specimen had been pacified and requesting extraction. But I did. Whatever I saw in the ice was how he'll free himself of this desolation. Without me.

Seven years. Seven years in this wasteland, bound to an unbreakable contract and receiving just enough supplies to keep us alive. Expanse was quick to decline our requests for rotation, and any concerns we raised regarding our mental wellness were brushed aside. We excavated the wind-blasted northern slopes and pored over barren scans of the planet's surface with nothing to show for it. We knew our well-being was not their priority, but we remained obedient. With no transport off the planet, what choice did we have?

We surveyed this small frozen world a hundred times over for the life-form Expanse Medical insisted was here—for it was our only key to escape. Whatever it was, it held DNA they thought was precious.

Now I see that Khatri was their lapdog all along. He had finally found what they wanted, and his reward was home. He must have hoped I'd be blind to it. Now, all I can think of are ways to thwart the man.

Every night through my window, across the snow-swept yard, the fluorescent glow of Khatri's lab taunts me. In a plume of cigarette smoke, with a bottle of bourbon in hand, I laugh at the man's naivety and at myself for ever trusting him.

I just wanted a friend.

No, I *needed* a friend, but I never really trusted him, nor anyone else. The seven years of comradery he showed me were just a ruse, so I'd let my guard down and think nothing of his clandestine behavior. The young, decorated biochemist secretly looked down on me like everyone else in my life. The stories he told me about his family and the daughter he longed to meet were probably all lies. As the years went by, part of me actually saw him as a friend. Now I know I never should have trusted him.

I can hear him tinkering away in his lab every night, after he thinks I've gone off to bed—always the same muffled sounds of chiseling and cracking ice. But tonight is different. He slips a note under my door urging me to use my hibernation pod so I won't be bothered by his noisy equipment. With a smirk on my face, I crumple it.

The distant noises of ice-work go late into the night, then abruptly stop. A raspy, gurgling shriek echoes across the frozen tundra. It quickly vanishes—yet, the cry permeates through me. I grab my parka and sidearm and charge into the whiteout.

Over the howling wind, I hear the cry again. As I approach the cold-storage outside Khatri's lab, the smell hits me first—blood. Through the window of the steel freezer door, I see a thin, skulking form with ice dripping from its sinewy body. A good seven feet of lean muscle, it paces back and forth erratically in front of a thick exterior door, sealed tight against the storm. Bright red blood drips from its claws and gaping mouth; its eyes like black marble watch my every move. The blinking red switch on the door indicates that the vault has been sealed.

I follow a trail of blood that leads into his lab. Khatri is slumped at his computer station, his right arm a mangled stump. A sidearm lies on the desk and his lifeless hand rests on a keyboard. Two luminous messages fill the screen.

I think to spit on the treacherous bastard, but my eyes catch the words. One is a message to his wife and daughter, expressing his love and regret. It tells of how he tried to come home, but could not, because he was no longer the man they loved.

The second message is for me. It seems unfinished, but wishes *his friend* a brighter future, one far from the shackles of this corrupt operation. He begs me to understand why he didn't involve me, and hopes that this "gift" to Expanse Medical is everything they'd ever dreamed of.

My eyes and face feel warm. The taste of salt coats my lips. I look at Khatri's message to his family one more time and click *Send*.

The room begins to rattle. Lights shine through the dark blizzard and flood Khatri's laboratory. Outside, the yard becomes a whirl of snow as a drop ship touches down.

A ramp is deployed and a group of unarmed men hurry out, a large container in tow. I seal the lab door as my eyes move to the cold storage manual-unlock on the desk. I think to give these men what they came for. It's the least I could do for a friend.

PRETTY GIRL

The quiet country road shifts like a ship at sea; Ilka tilts the opposite direction to regain balance. She accidentally overcorrects and a cloud of dust whooshes around her as she plops down onto the dirt.

It's the perfect vacation weather—warm with a hint of a late summer breeze that swishes the fields of tall tawny grass. Between the sun's hazy glow and the three grapefruit mimosas she indulged in at the restaurant, Ilka feels like a drunk cat, ready to curl into a ball for a nap.

If only these bags weren't so heavy.

Glurg, blurg. Ilka pokes her stomach with a freshly manicured finger. The hearty rack of lamb and bacon-roasted leeks she had earlier aren't going to cut it. She's hungry again, but the house is still so far away. The sobering thought forces her up. The decision to walk the three miles to town felt like a good idea this morning, but she regrets it now.

As if on cue, the rumble of an engine putters in the distance behind her, momentarily drowning out her hunger pangs. There's no one else on the road but her. Without turning, she quickens her pace.

The sound grows louder until—*beep beep*—"Hey, pretty girl, you need a ride?"

The moped driver slows to a crawl to match her scurrying walk. Long wavy brown hair snakes around his face. "Why the frown? You're too pretty to be sad."

Another man in the sidecar leans over the front wheel to grin and wave. His eyes sweep up and down her frame like a rodeo judge appraising cattle.

Ilka smiles until it hurts, and shrugs, pretending she can't understand. Facing forward again, she continues on her way. Her growling stomach tightens into knots, unfurling and curling around each other.

"Whoa, wait a minute. What's the hurry?"

Ilka can't tell who is talking and doesn't bother to look. The engine whines, revving to pick up speed. She almost lets out a breath of relief. Instead, the man spins the moped around to block her path and she lurches to a stop. The glass jars of honey in her bag clink together.

Their playful smiles are now predatory—or were they always that way? She begins to sweat, dizzy from neither the sun nor the drinks. Her stomach burbles and she strains to hold back her hunger. Now was not the time or place to think about food.

"That's not a nice thing to do. We were just being friendly, weren't we?" the driver says to the other. They both laugh as if it's an inside joke that they've told time and time again—a secret that only men like them share. He turns back to Ilka. "Think you're too pretty for us in those tight pants and titty shirt?"

Ilka looks down. Her jeans are scuffed and frayed with holes at the knees. Her yellow shirt is loose and thin, and, yes, unbuttoned just above her bathing suit, but hardly anything she considers a "titty shirt"—not that she would think of any shirt that way. She narrows her eyes at their leering faces.

"Well? No apology?" the driver says, turning off the moped. He scuffs at the dirt, creating a little cloud around his foot like a bull waiting to charge. The friend brushes his hair back with one hand and slow as a fox hunting a rabbit, climbs out.

Ilka drops her bags and runs into the field beside her.

Glurggg blurrrrggg. Her stomach grumbles fiercely, yelling at her to feed it. She ignores it. Impossibly tall stalks surround her on all sides, blocking everything from sight.

The sounds of crunching grass grow closer and closer.

She screams as her head whips back—one of the men has caught her by the hair. He pulls hard and she falls against a panting body that pins her arms at her sides. The other man steps in front of her and starts to claw at her buttons and zippers.

"Stop. I'm warning you," she says, her voice even against the sounds of their savage glee. Rage bubbles forth, frothing at the surface of her skin. The one in front of her pauses to dip forward and smirk. His breath his hot and smells like rancid meat.

"Oh, that pretty little mouth *can* speak?"

"Yes, but the others don't bother," Ilka says. The knots in her stomach release. A legion of ravenous tentacles spring forth from her belly. Each huge mouth is filled with rows and rows of pointed teeth that clack as they grow wider and wider, until some could swallow a melon whole.

The men screech and try to scuttle away. One tentacle shoots out like a viper on a mouse and latches onto the driver's throat, while a second clamps down on his friend's face with a hearty crunch that drowns the man's cries. The other tentacles follow one after the other, attaching with loud squelches, until they all find fleshy bits to chew in silence—save for a slurp here and there.

Ilka watches, baring every tooth, feasting until she's full. Her palate is usually more refined these days, but sometimes, eating junk food can't be helped.

IN PULSE

You ask for something to help you sleep because the shadow is fitful. It plays a kaleidoscope behind your eyelids at night, bright colors that you can't get rid of and aren't able to defend against.

Over-the-counter pills don't work, so you go to a chemist for something stronger. He thinks for a bit, goes far back into his store of small bottles, and draws out an ornate silver flask with a cork stopper.

"Make sure you only use it when you can sleep uninterrupted," he says, handing it over to you. "Otherwise it might be dangerous."

You agree. Easily. Anything to keep you from overthinking yourself and your stupid, fleshy body and how it can be so ungainly despite your best efforts. To finally avoid calculating every move because you cannot understand the people around you and the fluidity with which their thoughts and fancies change every other moment.

Because when you do fret, that's when the shadow is the loudest.

You don't want the shadow gone, you want it to be quiet. After all, the shadow was the first thing to ever love you.

You don't know how it got into your head. You just woke up one day and it was there: a dense darkness nestled at the base of your skull. It's hungry and wrathful and doesn't know what it wants much of the time, but it loves you all the same.

Don't let them treat you like that, it whispered when you were young, when they knocked you down into the tanbark and you got bruises on your elbows and splinters in your palm. *Tell them to stop.*

You're not sure what appeases the shadow—it seems to whisper less when you're happier, but you're not sure what makes you happy and what makes you sad.

Most days, the shadow is quite tame, yawning during your meetings and perking up at the odds and ends of gossip around your cubicle. But sometimes it grows restless, throwing things and slithering into your hippocampus, playing with your senses, turning orange to blue and bringing darkness where there had been none. It appears when you are a little heartbroken or your face burns with humiliation at what should have been an inconsequential slip-up. These things happen. But then the shadow gets angry, fuzzes up your dendrites and does questionable things to your neurons so that it's impossible to get through the rest of the day.

Your friends ask why you can't focus. You want to tell them, but it's weird to blame a shadow wreaking havoc in your head.

Sometimes you're tempted to let the shadow do what it wants. Maybe then it would quiet itself down. But you fear what might happen.

You hope the medicine will work.

The first few nights go well. You time it perfectly so that you are either asleep or able to remain in bed until the hours are up. Then you go about your day.

But hours slip, as they do. You can't always make it home in time, or you miscalculate your tasks. Sometimes you take your pills too late at night. In the morning, when your mind is exhausted and you're struggling to fight through the day—that is when the shadow pounces.

It is your turn to be the spectator in the back of your own mind, watching helplessly as the shadow walks around in your skin. It is belligerent, shameless, saying everything you would never say.

And yet, it is tamer than you thought. It drinks and laughs and dances, but isn't lustful or murderous, and in time, it lets you come back to yourself.

Why do you do things like this? you ask helplessly, appalled at how easy it is for the monster to do as it pleases and how the results can be so satisfying.

I do things like this because you hold back, the monster tells you, speaking into the mirror all matter-of-fact. *You hold back what you could be, how you could be.*

But I won't, you cry out. *I'm not as harsh as you.*

You call that harsh? the shadow asks incredulously. *I am forward, occasionally rude, occasionally terrifying, but your standards are quite low for what you could be. What I could be. If anything, I am less dangerous than you. I do not allow my aggression to build up and control me the way you do. If you did not hold back so much, you would not fear losing your grip.*

What do you suggest I do? you ask, cheeks flushing.

Let me out when you need me, says the shadow. *When I start to shout, you'll know that there are other ways.*

Why should I? you ask, even as the answer is already forming in the dark.

There is nothing sneering or smug in its reply. *Then I won't be so heavy,* it says. *You will say what needs to be said and be who you want to be. You will be happier, and I will be quieter.*

There's a logic to that, you must admit. You agree.

The shadow smiles within you, and your mouth curves upward.

HORSEPOWER

Evening, folks. Have a seat anywhere you like. Coffee? Don't want you falling asleep at the wheel. That's right, proper diner here—open twenty-four-seven, three-sixty-five.

Yep, bit eerie out there. Mountain casts a heck of a shadow, 'specially at night. But it's just the dark playing tricks. Ain't nothing out there gonna hurt you, long as you mind your manners. Can I getcha anything to eat?

Two burgers with the works, coming up. Hmm? Ha! Depends what you mean by *weird*. This's the only place open for miles—figure they call it a mountain pass 'cause folks pass right through. You're bound to see some strange things wandering in out of the dark. But, like I said, long as you're polite and keep to yourself, you won't find any trouble.

The *strangest* thing? Well, that's hard to say, but I remember the last one clear as day.

We get familiar faces now and then—folks running a route, night owls from towns a few miles down, the like. One night, pitch black as this one, this sweet thing named Brianne wanders in. Been by a couple times. Doesn't talk much, all tattoos, and this fluffy white hair like she's some kind of albino. You can always hear this big old beast of a bike rolling into the lot 'fore she walks in. Figure she's a courier or some such.

So, she strolls in, sits down at the bar, takes off her gear. All but this black scarf with jack-o'-lantern faces on it. Remember that, now; that's important. She orders, polite as can be, then takes out a pocket watch and keeps peeping 'tween it and the window. Ain't nothing out there but the trees and the old parking lot, so I figure she's waiting on something this time.

Now, there were other folks around that night. One of 'em, this boy Joshua, was sitting down the bar. Plain-looking guy— short brown hair, button shirt, nothing too terrible or inspiring. Thing about Josh: he fancies himself a smooth talker. Always shows up when he can't snag a date 'fore the bar a town over closes. He's here a whole lot, but that revelation never seemed to penetrate his thick skull.

I go freshen up some mugs, and when I come back, Josh's sidled up to her seat. I think, *Oh, dear, he's gotten too big for his britches.* First thing outta his mouth is "Aren't you hot?"

Brianne's rightly surprised—eyebrow shot up like a spring. "What?" she says.

Gotta give the boy credit, didn't faze him a bit. He points at her scarf and says, "Bit late for Halloween, though. Take it off and stay a while."

Oh my, did he look impressed with himself—even got a lewdy little wink in there. Brianne wasn't of the same mind. Gave him this long look and said she liked it.

That's all—just "I like it," but you could hear the hard in her voice.

Her order was up, and when I turned around to grab it, he said he could take the scarf off for her if she was having trouble. Couldn't believe my ears! I told him to mind his business when I dropped off her eggs. Barely get the words outta my mouth 'fore Brianne says to Josh, "You don't want to do that," sharp as a knife.

Didn't rustle him, of course. He laughed and said he was joking. Brianne went back to looking at her watch and wolfing down her eggs. I had more plates to run, so I left it at that.

I heard Josh saying some this-that-or-the-other while I dropped off everyone else's order, but I didn't have to hear it proper to know it wasn't going anywhere. Thought I saw her slap his hand away, but I had a table wanting extra sauce and saying they had a hair in their grits, so I couldn't babysit.

Josh was gone by the time I got 'em sorted, but I didn't notice that too much 'cause Brianne was acting all jumpy, staring outside. Threw some money on the counter and grabbed her things and went running out the door like the tax man was after her. Thought the glass would bang clean out!

Now, that's when I hear the bathroom door open and Josh comes running by, swearing a blue streak. Guess he hadn't given up hope, 'cause he goes chasing her out the door. I think, *Shoot, we're about to have a situation,* so I hustle after.

It was dark as a bat's ass out there, dark as it is tonight. Only had the light from the front windows to see by, and what do I spot but Josh catching up to Brianne. She's jogging into the dark, too busy pulling on her coat to notice. Just as I stepped out, he got a hand on that scarf of hers and pulled.

I don't know what he was thinking, but I figure he wasn't expecting her head to fall off.

God's honest truth, her noggin bounced right off and rolled through the gravel while the rest of her crumpled. I can still see her little puff of hair fluttering in the dirt. Josh starts screaming, falls on his ass and scrambles away.

Gotta say, I was a mite surprised when the rest of her stood back up and grabbed her head.

Right then, this other bike comes roaring down the road—couldn't see it out in the dark, but you could hear it screaming past and see the taillights disappearing through the trees. Brianne's body lifts her head up so it can watch whoever it is speed off into the night. Lord, did that head swear up a storm. It was 'bout the strangest thing I'd seen in quite a while.

She sticks her head back on and turns on Josh, all "What's your problem?" and "You have any idea how hard it is to catch a soul that doesn't want to be caught?" A bit fouler than that, of course.

Josh's all slack-jawed and gravel-burned and doesn't say much. She finishes hollering at him and storms off into the dark—can't see hide nor hair of her—and I guess his pride made him brave for just a smidge. He stands up and has the brains to spit, "Yeah, run! Fucking *freak*."

Friends, it was silent as the grave out there. Then this ridged white thing, like a whip made of bones, shoots out of the shadows and wraps around his neck. I swear I could hear her growling in my own head: "Wanna know what happened to the last guy who crossed me?"

He got the tiniest scream in 'fore the thing jerked him into the dark. Her engine came on and I swore I heard hoofbeats in there, carrying off onto the highway, with fire for taillights. Never did see Josh again. Lesson in etiquette, I suppose.

Ah, leaving already? Barely even touched your food. Well, the road calls. Come back next time you're passing through—and, remember, mind your manners. You never know who you're gonna meet out there.

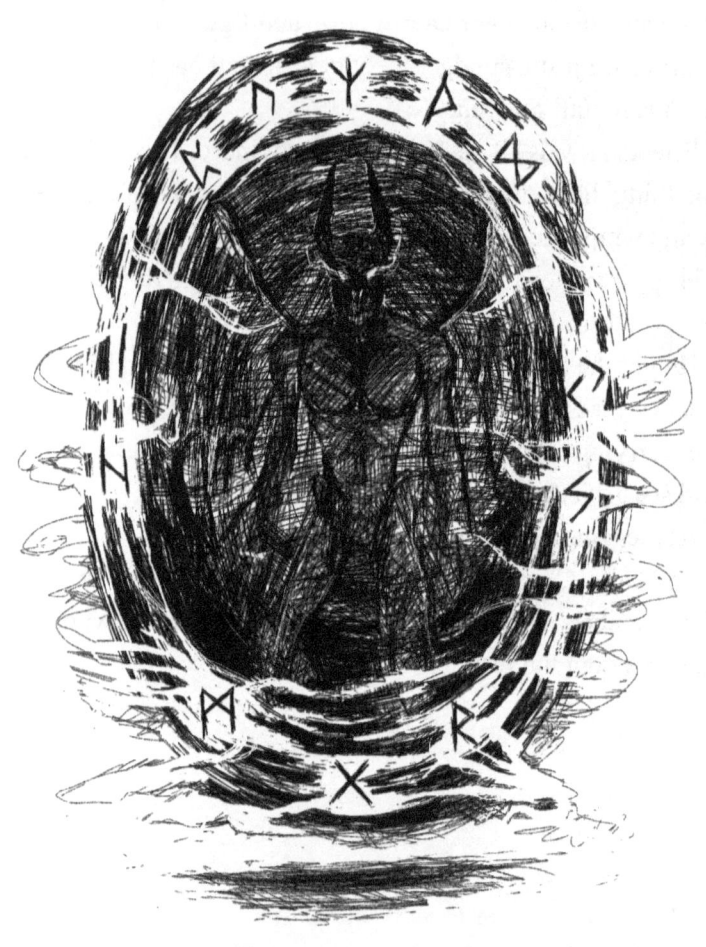

WELCOME TO DUNGEONS 101

"So the wizard explodes my door, tries to kill me and steal my artifact collection—which took over 200 years to complete! Scoured the world, different planes and realities and . . .

"Oh, sorry, Professor. Anyway, this wizard, he starts tearing my house apart, but his spells are total amateur hour. Tossed him through a wall, no problem."

As the creature tells its story, it becomes more agitated. Tendrils of steam rise from pores all over its enormous body. Its huge jagged wings flutter about, causing the candles in the room to flicker.

"But his adventurer buddies come in, think I've destroyed my own home and killed their friend! What do they do? Set the place on fire. No respect at all."

Murmurs of agreement ripple from the class of ten. Bil nods as one hand scrawls notes on parchment and the other two sit clasped in his lap. "Tell us what happened next, *Illegible*."

It sighs. *"I ate them."* Shocked whispers flutter through the room. *"What? They burned down my house trying to steal my stuff. It's still on fire! Eternally! Why is that always the go-to spell?"*

Bil frowns. "Technically, it isn't against our rules to retaliate if attacked, and killing in self-defense is acceptable on rare occasions." *Illegible*'s yellow eyes light up, until Bil continues. "But devouring out of anger doesn't count."

The demon wails at the podium. *"I'm so sorry. It happened so fast. Their stringy, bland bits didn't even taste good."*

Bil walks over and reaches up to pat *Illegible*'s burly arm. "You're here now, and that's what matters. We don't blame you. We all know adventurers never use doors properly."

Illegible smiles the best it can with a swirling vortex of smoke for a mouth and wipes away steaming snot.

"Next time, you can try using the 'Five Adventurer De-escalation Techniques,'" Bil says. "Let's practice right now."

Illegible nods, closing its watery eyes. Before it can recite Step One, the candles around the room begin billowing, their flames changing color, casting the cobblestone walls in blood-red light—a warning that the castle's defenses have been breached.

"Everyone, stay calm," Bil says. But his words are lost as the classroom's heavy wooden door splinters—once, twice, three times—until the edge of a great-axe appears through the gap.

Bil moans. "There's a damned handle!"

The axe wielder continues chopping, spraying bits of wood everywhere, until a scraggly, bearded warrior-sort pops his massive head through the opening.

"By the gods, it's a ritual sacrifice chamber! Monsters, everywhere!" He turns and yells, "Ready yourselves!" then continues hacking.

Another voice responds with loud chants. Dust falls from the ceiling as the ground rumbles. The room shimmers as its safety enchantments weaken.

The class scrambles out of their seats, throwing confused looks at Bil. He rubs his horned temples. "Just when we were getting somewhere," he says, then motions with his third arm for the group to stand behind him. A whorling blue portal ringed with flashing red runes appears. "Alright, class, through the emergency escape. Single file, no pushing—I saw that."

Everyone shuffles in one by one, grumbling about how much easier it would be to "lightly maim" the intruders. *Illegible* is last. *"Professor?"*

"There's something I must do first. Go on now."

Illegible shrugs and hunches over, disappearing into the portal.

The entryway remains open, hovering just behind the weary instructor as he conjures a camouflage shield. The warrior soon bursts in, twirling his axe, screaming unintelligibly. The oaf is smashing all the furniture he can, when another adventurer enters—a wizard, Bil infers from her flowing robes.

"Gron, you said there were monsters," she says, waving a gnarled staff around the room. "There's nothing but empty chairs and . . . are those cookies?"

Gron holds one, about to chomp down, when the wizard slaps it out of his hand. "They're probably baked with the blood of children!" He gasps and grinds it to dust with a sandaled foot.

Bil rolls his eyes and mutters, "They're chocolate chip."

An elven archer somersaults into the room, sweeping the area with a drawn bow. "Something is near," he whispers, gesturing toward a dark corner.

"Reveal!" shouts the wizard, pointing her staff at the shadows.

Nothing happens. Behind them, Bil exhales loudly and unveils himself. "Hello, there."

They all jump and turn. The elf shoots a volley of arrows as the wizard launches a fireball at him. All their attacks bounce harmlessly off Bil's shield.

As the smoke wafts away, Bil clears his throat. "Now then, perhaps we can discuss this . . . "

But a roaring Gron charges forward. The moment his great-axe lands, Bil's shield responds with equal force. The warrior flies backwards onto the others, knocking them to the ground.

"He speaks?" Gron says, rubbing his backside.

The wizard struggles to her feet and shines her staff at Bil, only to immediately recoil. "That's the Bil'nrok!" she hisses. "We must raze this haven of evil and flee. No one has survived an encounter with this foul creature."

"Then where do the stories come from?" Bil says, throwing all three arms up in exasperation.

Gron scratches his beard with a meaty hand, and mumbles, "He might be onto something."

The wizard glares at Bil, opening her mouth to respond, but the elf interjects. "We mustn't answer its riddles! What if it means to trick us?"

"Hrmm, it's not attacking. Maybe it's friendly?" Gron asks.

"Quickly, he's already fallen for its ruse!" the elf cries out.

"Yes, once again, our *mighty warrior* has fallen prey to evil." The wizard silences Gron's protests with a binding spell; his arms lock against his body as if bound by rope, while his mouth hangs wide open, frozen in mid objection. "Gather kindling—I'll begin the eternal cleansing fire for this wretched place."

"You'll what?" Bil shouts.

Ignoring him, the wizard begins chanting as the elf piles broken chairs in the middle of the room.

"Well, I tried," Bil sighs, and waves a hand. The ground beneath the duo shudders and falls away, and they tumble into a dark abyss. Shadowed seams seal, cutting off their echoing cries.

"Did you . . . kill them?"

Bil starts and turns; *Illegible*'s head is poking through the portal, its face scrunched in confusion.

"What? No, my dear demon. They're simply in a dungeon where they'll be crawling for hours looking for imaginary treasures, solving pointless puzzles. There's a way out, but it will take some time to find. They'll be fine."

Bil nods toward Gron. "As for him, there's hope. Like there is for us." With a snap of his fingers, the binding spell dissipates.

"I think I understand now," *Illegible* says, nodding.

Bil beams and claps two hands together. "Fantastic! I still need to explain the requirements for your essays on the proper responses to adventurers . . ."

His chittering floats away as he follows *Illegible* inside. The portal shrinks into nothing.

Gron sits in silence, eyes wide, chest heaving. But he shrieks as a plate materializes in front of him with a note on top. Written in elaborate script, it reads, "Chocolate chip, only. Enjoy."

Gron scratches his beard, then reaches for a cookie.

EXTRACTION

It was day three of the siege, and there was nowhere else to run from the neon fog. As the radio sputtered updates on the colonists' evacuation, Gibson inhaled through his gas mask, but the putrid fumes could not be stopped.

He stared in confusion at an eruption of short black spines protruding from his gloved hand.

"Another swarm!" a soldier cried over the pop of gunfire.

Gibson turned his attention to the bug-like shapes emerging from the mist. Grabbing his rifle from the muddy trench floor, he spotted Cortez huddled in the corner, staring at her right arm in horror. As Gibson approached, he saw her flesh pulsing.

"On your feet, private. Outpost Beta is still counting on us." Gibson grabbed her by the arm and pulled her up. Together they joined the line of soldiers against the foxhole wall. Three days ago these people were mere teenagers— the children of miners and farmers. Now they were a militia, and Gibson had been charged with buying time for their loved ones to escape. But as he eyed the mist and the swarm scurrying within it, not a hundred yards from the meager sandbags that shielded the unit, Gibson wasn't holding out hope.

Loading his last clip, Gibson looked over his shoulder, behind the trench. Through the clear air, he spotted the last group of colonists boarding escape pods. His wife and boy were in there somewhere.

With a deep breath, he whipped around to face the oncoming horde. His rifle hummed to life, its roaring joining those of his squad. Ahead of them, bullet-riddled alien bodies were stacked higher than the sandbags, their barbed appendages tangled into bloodied knots of arachnid flesh.

The fog's tendrils scurried over the field like the legs of the army it led, and with it came the stench of rotten flesh and charred bone.

With every breath he took, Gibson felt himself changing faster. Tremors shook his arms, throwing off his aim. Glancing down, he could see his veins bulging. Or were they veins at all? Lines seemed to wiggle beneath his skin, undulating as he breathed.

His rifle hummed; the ammunition indicator blinked red. Empty. The urge to turn his weapon on his own soldiers had ripped through him. He was grateful his gun was now useless.

But he knew they would soon be fighting the commands of the hive mind, too, if they weren't already.

"Hold the line, Gunners. Remember your training—don't give in to these bastards!" Gibson commanded. The raspy voice that emerged was not his own.

As he lifted his eyes, he saw two dozen soldiers hugging the trench wall, weapons still firing. But they weren't the young men and women he'd led into battle. Their mouths frothed like they were rabid beasts. They taunted the enemy with deep, demonic voices. Their bodies writhed, strange growths and appendages erupting like spears from their backs.

Gibson began to cough. The shell of his own body armor was beginning to crack from the inside. Blood trickled from his mask. A billow of neon spores spurted from his respirator. At last, the thick, radiant fog had completely engulfed them. All he could see of his gunners were silhouettes of squirming limbs.

Gibson could hear every crack of bone and the splintering of body armor. He could feel the growling from his soldiers. The lingering smell of human blood was the strongest sensation of all.

When his radio stuttered on, its screech was almost unbearable.

"Come in, Sergeant Gibson, this is Outpost Beta. The last of the colonists are on board the escape pods. Fall back to the extraction point!"

It was the transmission he had been waiting to receive for three days.

"Negative. Squad compromised. Proceed with evac. Gibson, out." With that, the last vestige of his voice disappeared.

Objections crackled through the radio as his headset fell to the shell-littered ground. He salivated at the sweet smell of human flesh in the air. It was close, but fading.

Through a break in the brilliant shroud, he saw a dozen bulking silhouettes take off into the clear skies above. Gibson's feeling of relief quickly died. He salivated as he began searching for remnants of humans with renewed purpose; extraction was no longer his mission.

BLOODLINE

Thunder masked the screams of the small pink demons as she sliced them with her mighty claws. The great horned creature watched as their bodies fell lifeless to the forest floor in a heap of cloth and broken weapons. Shouting in the distance told her many more were on the way. They had finally come.

The beast crashed through the underbrush towards her young, taking no time to mask her trail. A fiery pain pulsed beneath her thick hide, her fur matted with blood. The thorns from her attackers dug deep, reminders of a cattle hunt gone terribly wrong.

This time, they had been waiting for her with weapons and wolves. They caught her scent and there was nothing she could do.

The dense woodland soon gave way to open field. Fallen trees and cleared earth told her she was close. With her one piercing eye, she saw the cluster of wooden demon nests at the far end of the clearing, her snout picking up their foul scent. The familiar cries of their young, fearful of the midnight storm that pulsed overhead, carried with the wind. A flash of lightning revealed a swarm of the demons pouring into the field with burning branches and sharp sticks raised high. She lurched forward, running on all fours through the mud and heavy rain.

She was slowing. The throb of her wounds cut deep. She longed for the taste of elk to give her strength, but the sweet aroma of that flesh was but a distant memory. The demons had long ago hunted them all, and it wasn't long before they turned to preying on her kind instead. They had spared none, not even the young.

The storm ceased as she reached her cave, the tempest now only a gentle patter of raindrops. The cries of her twins echoing within the den drew her focus. Pain forgotten, she darted inside, gently collecting their small forms that were wrapped in furs. They had to leave before it was too late.

When she emerged from her cave, the cover of night had vanished, illuminated by countless torches. The demons had encircled her home, their shiny sticks pointed at her with the promise of biting pain and death. She held her twins close, arms trembling, and looked down into their round, bright eyes.

The demons' shouts grew louder. The whistling of their thorns cut the air, tearing into her flesh. Falling to her knees, she caressed her children one last time. The warmth of their soft pink cheeks filled her with a fleeting joy as she laid them gently on the ground. Their scent was pleasant. No demonic hate or evil tainted them like it did their sires.

She was the last of her kind. But maybe, years from now, these babies would tell tales of her and the love she had shown them. In her last moments, the thought made her feel whole.

POLYPHONY

Kostas marched briskly toward the church, pulling his hood tight as flecks of rain tapped against his forehead. A glance at the storm clouds crawling across the sky told him the rain wouldn't be gentle for much longer. He was moving so quickly that as he reached the church's front doors, he nearly trod on the gasping mound of feathers sprawled across the threshold.

A wing twitched, bare on one side. Plumes on the bird's back were slicked with blood and its head curled into its breast. Its small body shook with every ragged breath.

Setting down his satchel, Kostas kneeled to lift the creature and saw its bruised human face.

The boom of thunder filtered through miles of fields and forests to reach his village, the ground shivering beneath his feet.

He barely noticed as he staggered back, watching the creature wheeze on the clay path.

He should have left it. Taken a spade to it. It was surely not long for this world, and that would have been a mercy. But instead, with shaking hands and a turning stomach, he delicately lifted it and carried it inside.

The next evening was quiet, warm and soft, the air clean from the rain that battered the church roof all through the night. He felt a sudden longing for music.

He brushed dust from the harpsichord in the corner of the church—a lucky find, for he could not perform the traditional chants—and took a seat on its bench. He felt his soul settle as he played, notes trilling across the strings.

There was a sound like the wind settling in the casement. The creature was there when he lifted his eyes.

He nearly tumbled out of his seat, his fingers slamming down on the keys. The creature had disappeared but a few hours after he brought it into the sanctuary, and though he'd tried to treat its wounds, he was sure it had wandered off to die. Yet, here it now stood, balanced on the strings inside the instrument, like it was no heavier than a feather. A feminine face sprouted from an owl's body, both free of injury, and stared at him with round, brown, human eyes.

He did not know why, until it ruffled and plucked a string with its clawed toe.

The note drifted over his shoulders and echoed against the rafters overhead. The creature sat back, weightless on the strings, and looked at him expectantly.

Kostas blinked back. The creature plucked another string, more insistent this time. Kostas' fingers moved, pressing the keys, for he had little idea what else to do.

The creature sat attentively. Kostas ducked his head to avoid its gaze.

He supposed it wasn't a bothersome request.

Kostas shifted his heavy satchel as he walked through the church's side door, trying not to jostle any vegetables from its hold. He was nearly to the front of the pews when he spotted the creature.

It stood stone-still at the front of the church, cast in stained-glass light: the image of an angel gazed unblinkingly down from a window above, wings of orange and crimson framing sunlit auburn hair. The creature, healthier and stronger for all its days here, looked on just as steadily, its round head tilted back.

It lifted its wings, and before his eyes, they grew. They spread and bent, the owl body stretching tall, a vile gurgle falling from its mouth as its bones popped and cracked into a new alignment.

Kostas stumbled back, a pew folding his knee. Onions tumbled from his bag and bounced off the wooden floor.

The creature—a new creature—whirled on him.

A woman met his eyes: that strange face on a human neck, dark hair tumbling over bare breasts and belly. But her arms were gnarled wings, her skin a sickly blue, her legs the bony limbs of a hawk.

She stepped toward him. He tripped over his own feet as he clambered away.

By the time he realized that she was smiling—a strange, toothy, terrifying thing—the grin had fallen from her face. Her brows curved down as her wings curled in tight across her chest. She looked over her bony shoulder to the angel, down to her own misshapen wings, and then to him, her brown eyes misting.

Slowly, her teeth clenched tight, and she let out an ungodly shriek.

With a mighty flap of her wings, she crashed through the window, raining shards of glass down from the front pews. They crunched under his feet as he stumbled forward and watched her soar into the darkening sky.

Twigs replaced broken glass beneath his soles, cracking as he loped between trees as fast as his lungs could bear. He followed her shadow far, racing across fields and hills to the forest and the edge of the farmlands, but she had disappeared past thick black boughs.

Thunder rumbled a warning overhead, so low and loud that he nearly missed angry shouts skimming through the trees. But he couldn't miss the shriek.

A flap of wings and gleam of claws reached him through the trees. No—she had no claws. He tore past a last mahogany trunk and saw her towering over a pack of advancing men.

They shouted, voices a tangle, pitchforks and axes pointed like sabers. Farmers, who surely would have seen her shadow, too. She was larger, but they were greater in number, and even as she flapped her wings angrily, her hawk legs shuffled back.

With a screech, she leapt into the air, trying to lift away. An ax struck her in the back. The pitchfork pierced her wing to the ground as she fell. The men swore, whooped and swarmed as she howled in agony.

Kostas' breath pounded in his ears as he raced across the ferns. He wrapped his fingers around a farmer's shoulder and threw him aside. He saw a pronged fork rise through a cloud of feathers and wails, then crash down again, and again—

In the space of a step, he found it buried in his palm.

The farmers froze as if they had been struck by lightning. Kostas swallowed hard as warmth dripped down his shaking hand. The pitchfork wielder dropped the handle, ripping the weapon free; a silent scream poured from Kostas' mouth as pain shot in jagged bolts up his arm.

He found her at his feet when he turned—small owl body slashed and bloody, great brown eyes wide. Slowly, he kneeled down, wincing as he lifted her free of the greenery.

He heard the farmers muttering: *the church caretaker, the mute, why?* Kostas didn't look back as he marched through the trees, flecks of rain beginning to tap across the leaves underfoot.

He stumbled through the church doors, shivering under the weight of a torrential rain. Leaving drops of watery red on the polished church floor, he grabbed dry cloths and wrapped her tight, despite his throbbing hand.

He was no healer. When he swaddled her and collapsed onto the harpsichord bench, the cloth around her was stained with blood. Her wide eyes were half closed, her breaths labored.

Thunder cracked overhead, making him jump, and the harpsichord answered with its own shrill note under his elbow. He saw her eyes twitch open a fraction more, pupils shifting delicately. Slowly, he reached for the keys, leaving smears of red as he tapped out a melody with one hand.

Her breathing slowed as the energetic notes echoed through the pews, pushing out the sound of the pounding rain. He felt her claws moving gently, as if plucking at phantom strings. Her eyes turned up and met his through the water dripping from his hair.

He thought, perhaps, she understood. Perhaps he did, too.

TOXIC INFLUENCE

A minor attendant of no importance was the first to wear the mask in court. The king summoned Tilly Crown, his most trusted advisor, to explain its meaning.

"What sort of statement is this?" he demanded in his office, wondering irritably what faction was conspiring against him now and what steps he must take to correct it.

However, Tilly only shook her head. "It is not a statement, my king. From my understanding, he is obligated to wear it."

Though her information was usually accurate, the king was unconvinced. With the mask, the man became contrary, laughing at the king's decrees and conversation alike, his voice creaky like a squeaking door. The king issued a warrant of arrest to have him executed for treason, for to undermine the king was traitorous.

However, while the man died on the execution stage, it was not from the sword. The mask had a thick leather strap that fastened around the neck—to expose his neck for the sword, the strap had to be removed. As soon as it was, the man turned blue and fell to the ground.

Either way, the man was dead. Though the way it came about made the king uneasy, he paid it little mind.

Then two more courtiers showed up with the same sort of masks the very next day.

Irritated, the king summoned Tilly Crown back to the throne. "What is the meaning of this?" he asked.

"They say they have learned the same secret as the first," replied Tilly, ever reliable. "Or so they claim."

Like the first, though they did not directly contradict him, they refused to agree either. They kept the large insect-like eyes of the masks turned on the king: matte, fathomless, and eerie.

This time the king was less patient; he tolerated them for scarcely a week before bringing forth evidence that they had conspired with his enemies and leading them to the execution stage. Again, the men suffocated as soon as their masks were removed.

Four more courtiers showed up in masks the following day.

Within the week, the execution stage saw more deaths.

Within a day, masks appeared everywhere. They did not draw weapons or refuse their duties; they simply watched the king in silence, their glassy would-be eyes following his every move.

"What ails them?" the king demanded of Tilly in exasperation. "What great secret renders the very atmosphere intolerable?"

"I do not know, your grace," she replied. "I do not think it is something that can be shared merely by word of mouth. It must be believed."

The king, still angry, fell silent.

Now even the members of his cabinet were donning masks—the disease had reached the highest ranks of his court. They were men and women who couldn't be easily replaced, not when their expertise was so well-renowned.

"You cannot get rid of them," Tilly warned. "The realm needs them, and so do you, if you wish to remain king." Grudgingly, the king stayed his hand. The masks continued to spread, and he did nothing, alert though he was for signs of wrongdoing.

Word spread, and the king's brother came to court. He had inherited the land across the sea by marrying the heir apparent, and his realm had grown from kingdom to empire. From time to time on his campaigns, he sought his elder brother's aid in men and favors; this much, the king had refused, and though it was a move generally approved, there was the ever present concern of the brother's retaliation. While the reason for this visit was ostensibly to renegotiate a treaty that had stood for two hundred years, the king viewed it with suspicion, as did his ministers. On this point, at least, they still agreed.

When the emperor arrived, the king spent the day bringing him around the palace where they both grew up, a tour that was surprisingly hard on his legs and his lungs. Maybe, the king thought, it had to do with his brother's comments, his little smiles of condescension, and the general feeling that he was being sized up to be eaten. He was forced to excuse himself shortly after the dinner and retreat to his own rooms to catch his breath. He summoned Tilly to plan for the following day's negotiations.

When Tilly entered the room, he saw that now she, too, wore a mask.

In her hands was another mask, but different in style—an old-fashioned thing of iron with negligible eyes and a great long beak like the old plague doctors'.

"What is the meaning of this?" the king demanded, backing away as she approached. Even if his executions had long ceased, the rage at the betrayal welled within him, that the most loyal of his advisors would succumb to whatever reckless fever that infiltrated them all.

"It is your court's request," she replied. "We have a true problem to deal with, and your instincts have only led us astray. Your ministers have asked me to convey this message to you. They hope that you will be willing to join forces with your people to get rid of this threat, rather than fume and sulk.

"You are bad. He is worse. We have no interest in becoming his fodder. He sees weakness in our masks. If you come out with this mask, it will be a gesture of good faith, a display of unity that shows that personal loyalty and blind obedience should not be the only order of business. Perhaps, then, things will change from within as well as without. Will you do it?"

"There is no means to speak with that mask," he said, looking hatefully at it.

"There is—you will just have to think your words through first," replied Tilly.

"Why now? Why do you betray me?"

"It is a power of the mind—if you don't notice something, it isn't there. But I cannot pretend anymore, and I cannot advise a king who is toxic to me and his people. Consider it an advantage: All have known you are the king; now they will also know that you accept your people's needs. We need to present a united front, after all. What do you say?"

"There is only one answer, isn't there?" said the king, realizing that for weeks now, Tilly's face had been the only one he'd seen.

"There is," replied Tilly. "This is our will."

And so it was that the king muzzled himself.

WHERE DARKNESS LIVES

I rarely ventured out of bed so late and typically chose discomfort over leaving the warm glow of my nightlight. But that evening, my throat was the Sahara. Could I wait? Perhaps count sheep until I fell asleep again? No, it was impossible for my six-year-old mind, as the fluffy bastards continuously became sweet glasses of water.

Getting up from bed, bleary eyed and yawning, I peered out into the hallway's darkness. I shined my flashlight down the corridor; the beam was as bright as the yellow stars painted on my bedroom ceiling. Everything was where it should be: one small table on the right with antique lamp, bathroom door a bit further down, kitchen at the very end.

My little light had never failed me until that night.

Halfway down the hall, it flickered out, in, then died, the batteries clattering as I shook it. My eyes, no longer sleep-hazed, darted back and forth between the journey before me and the path back to bed. So few steps, but risky no matter which option I chose.

Slowly, the inky darkness crept in and surrounded me, until I was in a cave of nightmares. The flashlight, slippery with sweat in my hand, became hidden from sight. Even my body seemed to be gone when I looked down. I spun around and around, trying to get my bearings, but there was nothing but the dark. Which way? Which way was salvation?

Step-step-stop. The sounds of a light pitter-patter, like gentle feet on hardwood floor, reached my ears.

Step-step-stop. Step-step-stop.

Then . . . *step-step-step-step-step* . . .

I ran until I fell into bed sobbing. Between heaving breaths, I heard the footsteps fall away, back into the darkness of the hall.

I never left to get water again.

II.

Once, when I was eight, a storm had forced me inside during the day. As I paused from painting yellow dinosaurs to stare out at dull gray skies, a *click-click* noise arose, silencing my tuneless humming.

It was familiar. It was the same sound made when pulling the frayed incandescent light bulb string that hung in my closet.

It meant safety because my mother checked it every night. And each time, I had told her the closet door must always, *always*, be shut. But this time, it was different.

Click-click.

I looked around and saw that the faint daylight spilling through my room's two large windows died when it reached the closet. It completely cut off instantly like an invisible wall. Maybe no light could penetrate it. Maybe, like an endless hunger, the closet had eaten the particles as they drew near.

Click-click.

The bulb inside was dead.

With each empty click, the closet was taunting me. *Your light cannot stop me now.*

The darkness leached out, fingers crawling on the carpet, creeping steadily toward me. My legs coiled like a spring and I leaped over it, a shining Olympian high jumper. I saw it reach up with sharp black claws just as I dashed past my bedroom door and hastily slammed it shut. I could still hear it from the other side, seething in its defeat.

Click-click-click-click-click-click-click-click.

My mother replaced the lightbulb later that day. I always kept an extra one nearby, just in case.

III.

The last thing I remembered was a thin rope that hung from the ceiling in the hallway. Pulling it would cause a ladder to tumble out that led to the attic.

I never went up. I never walked under it, and hugged the walls to get by. I never even looked at the rectangular outline. I knew nothing good lived in there.

One day, the whole neighborhood had a huge garage sale. My parents took the opportunity to get rid of all the old junk we had in storage. They left the ladder down and the door wide open. It made it harder to avoid looking. I couldn't help but peek.

A dark maw gaped back. Like the closet, it seemed to inch toward me. But it didn't lunge. It beckoned, smiled even, dripping darkness from the corners of its mouth.

The black wisps that oozed out curled around my face, torso, legs, then retreated back into the attic, saying, *follow and finally, you will see.*

I think I whispered, "See what?"

And it replied, *what has always been here, waiting.*

My instincts said "Run." But a part of me needed to know what had been plaguing my twelve short years.

It was like the darkness heard my warring thoughts. Its smoky tendrils wound around my hands, pulling me forward like a lost child. My body locked up, rigid as a walking corpse. If I wanted to stop, I knew I wouldn't be able to.

I placed a hand on the ladder and stepped onto the first rung, then the second, until the attic engulfed me.

It was a whole day before anyone found me. I was huddled in the middle of the attic naked, hands over my ears, eyes squeezed shut. My father said I was cold to the touch and my mother couldn't find my clothes.

Evil casts long shadows, as long as your memory will hold them. It's been years and I still haven't fully forgotten. I never told them what I saw—I barely know myself.

I've pushed these moments far away. But, every now and then, I find myself back inside that attic again, waiting and waiting to be swallowed whole, wondering if the dark will let me go.

INHERITANCE

I lied to the child from the day you left.

I know how you would have seen him raised: with love and a warm heart. But I see you in the boy. His compassion and trust in others seems to grow more each day. It's another reminder of what I lost when you left us. So I do what I can to snuff it out.

"Father, the people at court say that Mother loved us both. That—"

"They know nothing. She abandoned us when you were very young. You musn't forget that you can count on no one."

His face is always the same after he asks about you: downcast and sullen, his shaggy black hair obscuring his eyes as he shuffles away. I must strengthen him for the bitter truth of the world that you taught me so well.

Nine years have passed without you by my side. The days of festivals, tournaments, and balls left with you. Now there is nothing to celebrate. Happiness and a love for my people have been replaced with hate and distrust for all those around me. The boy must be raised to see the world as I see it. With my help, perhaps he will avoid such a pain that you brought to me that I still feel all these years later.

On his fifteenth name day, I bring him to a public execution. It will do him good.

The herald yells to the arid summer sky: "By the name of the Emperor, the accused are sentenced to death-by-hanging for theft from the crown's stockpiles."

The crowd is silent. I see the wide eyes of the five as they tremble upon the gallows. One of the women looks just like you.

The boy stands beside me as we peer down upon the courtyard and its growing mass of onlookers. "Father, these men and women stole bread to feed their children. You must spare them," he pleads. "If Mother were here—"

"It doesn't matter what your mother would have done. These people are criminals. To steal from our stockpiles is to steal from the Emperor himself. Let this be a lesson to the rest of the peasants. You will rule someday. Do not place such value on others."

I give the command, reveling in the cries from the crowd as the floor falls out from beneath the criminals. I make the boy watch until the swinging bodies have stopped writhing.

He is silent that evening. His empathy for the bottom feeders of our kingdom could only have come from you. I vow to try harder and tear every part of you from him.

A month after his twentieth name day, I give him a chance to prove his worth by receiving a diplomat from the eastern kingdom. With my health quickly declining, I hope that I have wiped you from his mind. We meet the foreigner in the sand-dusted gardens of the palace.

"With the rising threats in the north, my king believes only prosperity can come from a renewed alliance between our two nations. We hope to rekindle the union of our nations as was before the loss of your beloved mother and Empress. All we ask is for your aid should this threat ever arrive on our shores. You shall have ours in return."

The boy becomes pensive. His silhouette against blue skies reminds me of you. "There has been peace between our people since I was very young. I see no reason why an alliance cannot be reborn to help both our economies and our people prosper."

I rise from my seat in a rage. "We will not spare warriors to fight another's war. We've had no need for alliances for fifteen years. We have no need of them now."

The boy looks to me. He doesn't say a thing, nor does he have to. He continues before I can think to say another word. He is as defiant and bold as you ever were, and I am speechless as that reality hits me.

"You must forgive my father. My mother taught me the value of alliances, but more importantly friendship. Let the bond between our two nations stand strong for years to come."

I hear your voice in his. Even after all these years, it cuts all the same.

After years of shaping the boy as best I could, my attempts to teach him fell on deaf ears. He fought me to the end, challenging my decisions at every turn. But what hurts the most is that, to this day, he is still just like you.

He kneels at my bedside now, my aged hand in his. "I love you, Father, but the hate and misery you've brought upon the empire since Mother left now leaves with you." The boy pauses, looking to my weakening fingers. For the thousandth time, your eyes stare back at me. "I know you were always trying to erase your memories of her. But I remember how good she was, and it brings me strength, not anger. I'll carry that with me until the end of my days."

I try to speak, to curse the boy's ignorance, but a gasp is all that I can manage.

"I know the truth, Father. All these years you would have had me believe she'd abandoned us, but I know that she fell sick and it destroyed you. I want you to know that I knew all along."

He rises as my hand falls limp. My hearing is failing, but I catch a few words he calls out to the councilmen—change, peace, hope—and my eyes finally close.

HARVEST

Nights always look brighter now, as if I could reach up and pluck out a speck of space dust. I like to take long breaks and lie in the field, watching the stars float by; it's like gazing through an aquarium tunnel of the cosmos. Far above, warmth and light filter down from the latest supernova. Lush vines and flowers larger than my head instinctively turn up towards the glow.

Maybe it's a mixture of the starlight and the creature's breath, but food grows faster and tastes better than any we had before. We hardly need to eat anything to feel satisfied. Our life spans have been extended exponentially. And war, fallout, plague—they have all disappeared.

Before the beast swallowed Earth in a single gulp, we had nearly destroyed it. Then, without warning, and without knowing, we disappeared down a gullet and found ourselves in the belly of what we later christened the Worldbeast. It had sensed the premature death of our sun and like a moth to a flame, was drawn to its decaying energy and heat.

Through its iridescent hide, we watched our 4.5 billion-year-old star die. But Earth was saved. We were saved. And now there is balance.

Paradise and peace. It is more than we deserve. I often repeat this mantra to myself and the others. The least we can do is stop the contagions that could harm the beast and threaten the tranquility it provides.

Many went mad during the first Harvests. The work was too hard for them, but in time, we adjusted. It was the only way forward, and the Harvest is a small price to pay for all we have gained.

A soft, deep hum fills the air, stirring me from my reverie. The unearthly thrumming is our first and only sign that the Harvest to rid the beast of contagions has begun.

The sound of the bone blade catching cracks through the silence. Tall stalks of blue moongrass shiver around me as I shake the scythe loose from the contagion. No matter how much we cut down, there is always more the following year. It's hard work, but I enjoy being outside gulping down the sweet air.

I run my thumb against the bone scythe's edge. It hasn't been sharpened nearly enough. Quickly, I take a whetstone to it and smooth down the roughness. The hardier bit of the contagion's leg flesh had caught my blade earlier. Now it cries out as it tries to drag itself away, but the injury prevents it from crawling too far.

There is nowhere to go anyway. The planet is a creature suspended in sap. Yet the contagions somehow survive. This one will not.

I look up and the stars become a messy kaleidoscope as my vision blurs. Bone meets bone as I swing downward. A clean cut.

Paradise and peace, I whisper. My face is wet with blood, but I'm unsure why there are tears.

The Worldbeast's song is filled with lament and hope for the Harvest today.

ABOUT THE AUTHORS

Lily Prasuethsut is a jack-of-all trades, aspiring master of everything. She has worked as a writer and editor for various tech websites, was once editor-in chief of a Berlin travel guide, and acted as the marketing manager for a startup in Silicon Valley. From there, it was only a small step to short fiction and poetry magazines. When she's not running Minute Fiction, she can be found dabbling in Dungeons & Dragons, coding, painting or trying to write several novels that can't seem to complete themselves. Sometimes, she'll even venture into the Alaskan wilderness to hunt for berries, mushrooms and monsters.

Like Father, Abominable, Pretty Girl, Welcome to Dungeons 101, Where Darkness Lives, Harvest

Ashley Reed is a writer obsessed with asking questions no others dare, like "What's scary enough to scare a ghost?" and "Is online dating also terrible for monsters?" She has worked as an editor, copywriter, junior archivist, livestreamer and game designer. After incubating in the dark forests of Oregon for twenty years, she returned to her ancestral hunting grounds of California, where she remains to this day. In her spare time she haunts mysterious basements, quiet beaches, abandoned roller rinks and other odd places—all very informative for her writing.

The Serpent's Tale, Things that Go 𝄞𝄢𝄢 in the Night, Siren Song, Honey and Dates, Horsepower, Polyphony

Peter Corkey is a North Carolina native who loves the environment, sailing and retro gaming. When he's not expanding his collection of Nintendo memorabilia, he can be found watching *Game of Thrones* for the tenth time, or re-reading the series for the third time. His obsession with the fantasy genre can be traced back to his childhood where he wrote and illustrated stories inspired by the *Redwall* and *Narnia* books, as well as the Warcraft computer games. He likes to think his writing skills have improved a bit since then, and hopes to one day entertain readers with the novel he's currently working on.

Deep Down, Luca the Great, Hyperborean, Extraction, Bloodline, Inheritance

Nicole Ellis is an anthropologist by training and in practice, if not by trade. She has been writing all of her life, rooting her worlds in the fuzzy seam where the magic and mundane tend to blend together. When she isn't writing, she reads eclectically, plays video games, enjoys dancing and is slowly learning how to draw again. She can usually be found in the places where stories live, like museums, theaters and bookshops.

Neighborhood Rules, A Babysitter's Duty, The Dragon Cometh, The Spider Jar, In Pulse, Toxic Influence